THE GUARDIANS OF EARTH

OONA AND THE LUMINOUS BEINGS

ORIANE LIVINGSTON

Oriane Livingston
The Guardians of Earth
Volume 1. Oona and the Luminous Beings

© 2024 Ariane Éditions Inc.
C.P. 183, Saint-Sauveur, Qc, Canada J0R 1R0
info@editions-ariane.com
www.editions-ariane.com/en

Graphics and layout : Marquis Interscript
Cover illustration : Gabriella Barouch
Revision : Diana Halfpenny

Legal Deposit
ISBN : 978-2-89626-656-2
Library and Archives Canada, 2024

Nous reconnaissons l'appui [financier]
du gouvernement du Canada.

Canada

Printed in Canada

*To the Santa Monica Mountains
and Cosmos, my beloved husky.*

PROLOGUE

A white eagle flew swiftly through a sea of stars, as if eager to carry out an important mission. He drifted above the swirling disk of the Milky Way for an instant, then dove resolutely into its heart. Once in the center, the eagle suspended his flight for a minute to gaze at the miraculous vision. It was like discovering a precious gem.

The majestic Earth appeared behind white spiral patterns formed by vaporous clouds.

Since time immemorial, the ancient Earth has been the jewel of the cosmos, radiating beauty and harboring sacred secrets.

Behind the Mountain of the Moon, in the Earth's heart, lives Eterna, the Spirit of Earth and the source of all life.

At the beginning of time, every human lived in harmony with Nature and was connected to Eterna's heart by a filament of light.

Earth was a lush paradise and humans glowed with happiness.

But on a winter day, in a faraway galaxy, on a planet without a sun, the Dark Planet, jealous of Earth's beauty, severed the luminous threads, hoping to take over the source of beauty for herself.

A terrible battle ensued. Now disconnected from Eterna, humans turned on her and started to destroy Nature!

The Luminous Beings, a peaceful species from a more highly evolved universe, sacrificed themselves to infuse a crystal with their own light in order to restore the sacred filaments. This crystal is the Supreme Stone, Eterna's last hope of survival.

Only three children of the Luminous Beings survived, hidden somewhere on Earth along with the Supreme Stone. One of them is the Guardian of the Forests, another is the Guardian of the Waters, and the last one is the legendary Guardian of Earth.

Suddenly, melodic singing, gentle birdsong and the sound of flowing water rose into the air, emanating from the depths of Earth. The eagle bowed his head as he recognized the voice of Eterna, suffused with melancholy: "*N' gala kaet'. Nelh ap nehn nh'ilni nanih …*" [Our world is in peril. We feel it in our hearts. Soon, it will be too late …].

The eagle swooped toward Earth. He flew in circles in the cloudless, dusky sky that dwarfed Los Angeles. The feathers of the noble bird's glowing plumage formed a perfect geometrical pattern, nested inside each other like Russian dolls to infinity, and his kind, sparkling eyes reflected the continents of Earth. In the far distance, the incandescent sun was sinking into the ocean, striking its surface with iridescent purple rays. The majestic bird began to cough as he flew through smoke from chimneys and cars stuck in heavy traffic below: the grey fog of human civilization. His heart tightened, his eyes expressing a profound sadness.

A single feather twirled through the air, descended between the city's shining glass and steel monoliths, then gently dropped into the grass at the feet of a young girl wearing yellow sneakers.

CHAPTER I
"Once Upon a Time on Planet Earth ..."

Oona looked at the Milky Way through her telescope, hoping her star would speak to her that night. She was kneeling on the grass, captivated by the eternal spectacle of the galaxy. Oona had always been certain that there was a secret hidden beyond the world she knew. That there had to be something more than all this: an invisible giant holding the world, the sky, and the whole cosmos. Something bigger. The day before, she'd tried to get some clues from her new astronomy teacher at the very first weekly meeting of the Junior Astronomers Club, as they were building a model of the solar system together. Finally, someone who could answer her questions about all those orbs of light hanging in the night sky.

"Mr. Abrachaleus, how many planets are there in the solar system?"

"Well, there are eight planets that orbit the sun, which is a star. Mercury, Venus, Mars, Jupiter, Saturn, Uranus, Neptune and, of course, the Earth," her teacher replied, handing her a ping-pong ball.

At nearly eleven years old, Oona was the youngest of the club. Confused, she looked at the giant NASA poster hanging on the wall, showing the innumerable stars dotting the celestial vault.

"In all of space, there are only eight planets?" she asked, astonished.

"No, there are far more planets than that in space. They're called exoplanets. But today we're focusing on the solar system."

"And how big is space?" she asked, struggling to get the blue ping-pong ball to revolve around a paper mâché sun. The Earth seemed so small!

"The cosmos is infinite," he said in an affable, albeit somewhat condescending tone.

Carl Abrachaleus had curly gray hair and a goatee that reminded Oona of a billy goat.

"But just how big is it?"

"Well, it's enormous! The Earth is in the solar system, which itself is in the Milky Way, which is part of our universe," he declared.

By way of demonstration, the teacher twirled his hands in larger and larger ellipses around the miniature celestial objects rotating on thin metal wires.

"But what's after that?"

"After our universe? Well, infinity," he repeated, frowning and looking profoundly irritated. "So, there's no end. It doesn't stop."

"But … how can it not stop?"

"Look, if you're talking about our universe, the universe that humans can observe from Earth, well, yes, there is an end. And there are other galaxies and other stars after that."

"But what is there after all those galaxies and stars?"

The teacher rolled his eyes. For a minute, it looked like he might charge forward, like a bull.

"Well, it's complicated. Oona, let's just focus on today's lesson for now, okay?"

She'd told herself that this was the excuse of an adult who didn't want to admit his ignorance. And, while she waited to uncover the mysteries of the universe, she'd given herself a star in the sky, a star all her own. It was her secret. Unlike the other stars, the one Oona had chosen looked tiny, with a bright blue halo and only three points. Its celestial siblings were gathered in clusters, or rather in constellations, as Mr. Abrachaleus had just explained to her. Hers, however, was all alone, like an orphan in the night. "I'm adopting you!" she'd called out to the star, laughing, as if it could hear her. "And you? Will you adopt me? We'll keep each other company." Ever since that night, every time Oona was sad, she'd take refuge in her star, her second home. For several nights now, however, her star had been flickering strangely whenever she looked at it. *Maybe it was trying to communicate with her!*

In the garden, Oona kept her eyes on the star, waiting for the signal that helped her feel less lonely. She was distracted by the tickle of an ant climbing her bare leg.

"So, little ant, we're climbing up giants today?" Then she thought, *Humans are like ants who don't know there's a road at the end of the garden.* "Yes, we know!", the ant replied, annoyed. Oona gasped. Had the insect really just talked to her? No, impossible. It couldn't be! It must have been another figment of her vivid imagination. She shook her head, adjusted her headlamp, and drew a diagram of some constellations on a piece of paper. A long white feather, which had been lying at her feet, rose gracefully into the air. For a moment, it seemed to her that an aspen tree was swaying in the wind and polishing the stars overhead. *Nature is so beautiful, like a living painting!* she marveled, as she reached to grab the feather out of the air.

Suddenly, her headlamp stopped working. Oona pressed the switch several times, then tapped the bulb. Strange. She'd just changed the battery the day before. Then, a loud sound, like breaking glass, shattered the silence. Oona dropped her pencil and turned breathlessly toward the house at the end of the garden. She could feel her heart pounding in her chest and her star began to blink frantically, as if trying to get her attention. An enormous white eagle circled majestically in the glowing sky above Oona before swooping at dizzying speed toward her. She choked back a scream.

The supernatural creature stopped in mid-air, hovering right in front of her face. Their eyes met. As she gazed into his kind eyes, she saw all the Earth's continents and oceans reflected in his irises. For some inexplicable reason, Oona was not afraid. She raised her hand to touch the bird's feathers, to make sure that she was not dreaming.

But the voices from the house were growing louder. Oona hesitated to abandon the eagle, then ran to the back door of the house. She peeked through the window, then turned the door handle, trying to make as little noise as possible. As she entered, she could hear the sounds of an argument. A shiver ran down her spine and she involuntarily whispered, "Mom." Oona's legs felt like lead as she ran up the stairs to the second floor, then came to a halt in front of the door to her mother's room. Her parents had slept in separate bedrooms for as long as she could remember. Oona's eyes were already filled with tears, and they spilled down her cheeks as she cried out, "Stop, please stop arguing! I'm begging you, stop!". She stood, frozen in panic, in front of the door.

Hearing no reply, she ran to her room and hid under the covers, curled into a snail shape, with her hands covering her ears. Forcing herself to think about her star, she gradually drifted off to sleep, the eagle feather clutched to her chest as it rose and fell with her breathing.

CHAPTER II
A Bird in Distress

The next morning, Oona was still groggy as she grimaced and grabbed her glasses from the nightstand. As she sat up in bed, her elbow bumped the orchid next to her bed but she managed to just prevent it from falling. Then, with her miniature watering can, she sprinkled a few drops of fresh water onto its smooth leaves. The flower seemed to glow with a supernatural light. Oona blinked, rubbed the lenses of her glasses, and gazed at it in disbelief, but the plant had returned to its normal appearance. Enough daydreaming! She needed to make sure her mom was okay. There was a lump in her throat as she jumped to her feet and hurried down the hallway. It was completely silent. As she walked softly toward her mother's room, her heart felt heavy with dread. All this would end badly one day, she thought.

"Mom?" she said quietly, her mouth pressed against the crack of the door. Her legs were shaking.

"Yes, my dear?" her mother replied, encouragingly.

"Can I come in?"

Oona didn't wait for an answer and pushed open the door. Her mother had her back to her, and was busy painting a giraffe on the wall. It was wearing a pretty dress with purple spots.

"Mom? What are you doing?"

"I've always wanted to decorate this wall. Did you know that giraffes are also called 'camelopards'?" she asked.

Oona's mouth formed the word "No" but didn't make a single sound.

"Half camel, half leopard, see?"

Oona's heart sank as she watched her mother paint the animal's horns blue.

"Isn't today the day of your math test?" her mother asked.

Oona could see through her mother's words. She knew very well that she didn't want to discuss last night's events.

"Yes, it is. Are you sure you don't need anything?" Oona said, retreating into the corridor.

"No, don't worry, and good luck on the test, my little wolf!" she replied affectionately.

This was her mother's nickname for Oona, because she had a prominent canine that looked just like a real wolf's tooth.

"Okay, Mom. See you later."

Oona went back to her room and pulled on a loose T-shirt, a pair of sweatpants that were far too big for her, and a hoodie. A strand of her long auburn hair got caught in the zipper again. Because her father refused to pay for her to go to the hairdresser, her mother was the one who cut her hair, but it was always a disaster: she hid the resulting asymmetrical cut as best as she could under the hood of her oversized sweatshirts. This upset her mother, who tried vainly to persuade her to wear nicer clothes. It had been almost five years since her family had moved to the West Coast for her father's work. Oona had been thrilled about the change. She'd always felt like an explorer, and the prospect of conquering the Wild West promised to satisfy her insatiable curiosity, her need to experience and learn new things. Her imagination had been fueled by visions of cowboys in the desert, and she'd hurried to the library to devour every book about California she could find.

She tugged harder on the trapped strand of hair and suppressed a cry of pain. Got it! She'd managed to free it just as she tiptoed by the door to her father's room, which was at the top of the stairs. Hearing his radio, she felt a knot form in her stomach. She dashed down the stairs, grabbed her skateboard, and left.

Oona jumped on her skateboard and sped toward the bus stop. Little by little, the wind and sun chased her gloomy thoughts away and her heart felt lighter. She was thinking about the enormous white eagle she'd seen the night before when, suddenly, her jaw dropped in surprise. There was a baby bird standing right in the middle of the road, and it seemed to be staring straight at her. Oona had the strange feeling that the small, defenseless creature's thoughts were filling up her head and that she was able to pick up on its sense of utter helplessness. The bird's panic was mixed with total incomprehension: as yet unable to fly, the chick was jumping up and down on the asphalt and crying pathetically. Oona quickly shifted her weight to the back of her board to dodge it but lost her balance and fell backwards onto the road, her glasses flying into a nearby bush. Luckily, she spotted them right away and quickly put them back on. Sunlight illuminated the little bird's tiny wings as it kept trying desperately to fly away.

As if out of nowhere, the big school bus came roaring up behind them. The poor baby bird was still shaking on the pavement. The vehicle was getting dangerously close. Oona shouted "No!" with all her might and instinctively reached her hand out toward the huge wheels bearing down on them. She closed her eyes.

There was the sound of screeching tires and then …
complete silence. She opened her eyelids and cried out
in astonishment: the bus and its occupants were frozen
in place, just a few inches away, as if Oona's hand had
stopped it in its tracks. She got a hold of herself and
picked the fragile creature up, placing it carefully on
her palm.

"Shhh, shhh …," she murmured, stroking its head
to calm it while a flood of burning questions whirled
inside her head. *Did her hand stop the bus? That's
impossible, how could it be?* But nothing made sense.
The driver slowly emerged from her paralysis and
shook her head, confused.

The chick's little feathers started to sparkle with
strange patterns, leaving twinkling trails in the air as
it flapped its wings contentedly. Oona blinked in
amazement, then removed her glasses to check the
lenses. Her glasses seemed fine. Puzzled, she gingerly
placed the bird in the pocket of her sweatshirt and
prepared to board the bus.

CHAPTER III
A Chumash Boy

"Good morning, Ms. Daniels. Sorry, I mean 'Lady Galadriel'," Oona said deferentially to the school bus driver, a reference to the heroine of the *Lord of the Rings*, whom the driver worshipped.

Sitting behind the large steering wheel, Ms. Daniels was in her late fifties and wore her hair in a neatly coiled bun, like a 1940s Hollywood actress. She had plastered glamorous black-and-white portraits of herself on the inside of the driver's window. Clearly, Ms. Daniels had dreams of becoming a movie star.

"Hello Oona," she replied, fluttering her fake eyelashes. "You can call me Galadriel, friend of the elves," she added with a coquettish smile.

The bus was half full. Oona headed toward the back and sat alone by a window. Outside, the sun was shining high in the sky and the leaves of the trees, yellowed by heat, looked forlorn. The vehicle started back up and made its way along the western bank of the Blue River, or, more accurately, along the river's dry bed. The grass, which had originally been green, had turned pale yellow, and whole schools of dead fish had washed up onto the banks. Oona gasped, her heart sickened by this sad sight, and tears sprang to her eyes. Concerned for the little bird nestled against her chest, she made sure it was breathing and sighed with relief. Then, she grabbed her apple juice box, took a sip and placed the end of the straw inside the bird's beak. As it sipped the sweet liquid, the animal shivered with joy, reinvigorated. "I'll take care of you until you can fly", she whispered.

Next, she pulled a paper covered with notes out of her bag. In her journal, she'd written down the location of her star in the sky, along with the dates and times at which it had started to flicker, or, as she liked to think, to speak to her. She was hoping to detect a pattern. Then she'd be able to anticipate its messages and maybe even decipher its language! Perhaps her star had an important message for her that would give her some comfort. She glanced over at the bird. "I'll call you Cosmos, it's a poem in one word. 'Cos' rhymes with 'mos'!", she exclaimed, softly laughing to herself, before focusing her attention on the paper again. She was looking intently at her nighttime scribblings when some singing made her look up.

"Children, look to your right!" Ms. Daniels shouted into her microphone as she slowed the bus down. "Some Chumash people wearing their traditional costumes have gathered today for the Rain Dance. They're calling on the stars to cure the drought. No school for them today!" Oona quickly opened her window. Along the edge of the forest, a dozen Native Americans were performing tribal rain dances and singing. She was mesmerized by their feathered headdresses and brightly colored tunics. The air around them was distorted by the heat, making their performance seem like a mirage. It looked like a circle of majestic birds. Gazing in admiration, she almost burst into applause when, suddenly, something caught her attention.

"Quit teasing that dog!" shouted a young Chumash boy.

A group of children scattered and a lanky white dog that looked like a wolf escaped from its tormentors and bounded up to the boy, who appeared to be about twelve years old. He had a slender, athletic build, and was dressed in nothing but sweatpants and sneakers. Unexpectedly, Oona was overcome by a wave of unconditional love. She had the odd sensation that she could feel the emotions that the dog was experiencing as it jumped up on its master. *What was happening to her?* Just a few minutes ago, she had also been able to feel the bird's fear also. *Were the animals trying to communicate with her?* She chased these nonsensical questions from her mind.

Oona smiled as she watched the dog's joyful reunion with the boy. The adolescent had silky black hair on one half of his head, while the other half was shaved. Necklaces of turquoise beads dangled on his bare chest. He observed the rain dance with an air of noble detachment. Oona leaned toward the half-open window. Just at that moment, a breeze blew through the bus and carried her paper covered in scribbles outside. Helplessly, she pressed her palms against the window. The paper whirled in the air and landed on the boy's bare, tanned shoulder. He grabbed the paper and raised his head toward Oona. She had never seen such a handsome boy, and her pulse quickened.

Their eyes met and, at that moment, Oona felt something pass between them, a spark of eternity, as if they had known each other since the beginning of time. It shook her to the core. In her pocket, Cosmos chirped, as if in approval of her excitement. The boy started to run alongside the bus, trying to give the paper back to Oona, but the vehicle was going faster than he was. With her hands still pressed up against the window, she watched as the boy and the dog first faded into the distance, then vanished from sight. She could feel her cheeks burning.

Chapter IV
The Magical Flower

Oona stared at her mother as she stood behind the kitchen counter, waiting anxiously to see what she would do next. Why was her mom putting avocados and mustard in the blender? Was she going to add something that would mean she was following an actual recipe? Her mother added chestnut ice cream to the strange mixture.

"Mom, is everything all right?"

"Yes, everything's fine, dear. Did you see Albert?" she asked, opening an upper cupboard. Inside was row upon row of glass jars filled with American Airlines salt packets. Oona's father saved every condiment packet he was given when he was flying. One time, she'd even seen him take some bread rolls from his suit pockets. His motto: Why spend more when you can spend less?

"Albert?"

"Yes, Albert, our cat."

"We don't have a cat, Mom."

Her mother looked confused by this news. Oona pulled at the collar of her sweater. She was too hot, and the wool was prickly against her skin. Because she suddenly felt like crying, Oona took her math test and handed it to her mother, who stared at her daughter, her violet eyes contrasting sharply with her pale skin. She had been acting strangely for over a year now, but her odd episodes were increasing day by day.

"Well done! You're so brilliant and special! Don't let anyone tell you otherwise," her mother said, sprinkling coffee beans over her mysterious concoction.

Her father burst into the kitchen. Instinctively, Oona took a step backwards. Without saying a word, he brushed past his wife and daughter and sat down heavily on the sofa before turning on the television.

Balthazar Monroe was a colossal man with a stocky build and a thick neck. His hair was cut very short in a military brush cut, and he tended to wear tight-fitting suits. But the first thing people noticed about him were his eyes: two blue slits, intense and searching. A stony silence hung over the kitchen. On the screen, a journalist was relaying the latest data about global warming.

" … our planet's population has officially passed the ten billion mark and is drowning in its own toxic pollution. Temperatures have reached alarming levels. If we fail to act …"

"Guess who got an A on her math test today?" Oona's mother interjected.

Her father pretended not to hear, ranting into his beard at the reporter, who was advocating the use of electric vehicles.

"This idiot is going to jeopardize the Group's sales!" he muttered.

His daughter's achievements were clearly of no interest to him, but Oona was hanging on his every word.

"Well, it's your brilliant offspring!" her mother exclaimed.

Oona gave a faint smile and hunched her shoulders, unaccustomed to getting praise from her family.

"Did anyone get a better grade?" he growled.

"No, it's the best grade," Oona replied hurriedly, filled with hope.

"Why should I congratulate you when you could have done better?" her father asked, dismissively.

Resignedly Oona stared at the ground. Why had she allowed herself to hope? Her heart weighed heavily in her chest.

"My sunshine, what do you want to do for your birthday this year?" her mother asked.

Oona remained silent, glancing furtively at her father.

"Oona?" her mother repeated.

Oona took a deep breath.

"I wanted to go to the Animal Ranch."

"Ridiculous!" Balthazar exploded. "Why do you insist on celebrating the fact that you're a year older? When is your birthday, anyway?" he asked.

"In two days," she replied.

The universe seemed to waltz around Oona, unable to grab on to anything tangible. She had to constantly walk on eggshells around her father, while her mother made her think of a helium balloon that would fly away if she were ever to let it go and not keep bringing her back to Earth.

"And who's going to pay for this visit?" he inquired, sarcastically.

Her mother's eyes began to flash with anger.

"Come on, Balthazar. Don't be a Scrooge."

He got up menacingly. She flinched. Oona ducked behind her, clutching at her sweater. She felt her mother's fingers discreetly push her away and she slipped out of the room and ran up the stairs. Then she hurried to her room at the end of the hallway and locked herself in, sliding down the door until she sat on the floor. Paralyzed with dread, she remained perfectly still, trying to quiet her ragged breathing as she listened for the slightest noise. The blood rushed to her ears, and they started to ring. Her parents' voices grew louder and louder. Oona crawled inside a pyramid-shaped tent she'd made and sighed. She squeezed her trembling hands against her ears, her palms forming a bubble that isolated her from the rest of the world. The ringing was now louder than ever. Another fight. Her heart was being crushed by an anvil. Cosmos emerged from her pocket and let out high-pitched squeaks, then rubbed his feathers against her cheek. He must be able to sense *her* emotions, too! The little creature's concern warmed her heart, and, despite her growing anxiety, she could feel herself starting to smile. Looking up, the orchid on her nightstand caught her eye. She was glowing. The sounds of the argument merged into a strange melody.

Oona stared at the flower, which had begun to wilt. Her perfectly shaped petals were the color of freshly fallen snow and her natural grace reminded her of a prima ballerina doing an arabesque. The flower's exquisite fragility moved her. Gently, Oona touched the lifeless stem and collapsed, her face inundated with tears.

The outside sounds faded away as Oona disappeared into her inner world. When she opened her teary eyes, the flower's petals gleamed with a strange light and then … she came back to life and stood upright, as if resurrected by an unseen hand before her astonished eyes.

Stunned, Oona stared at the revitalized flower, which sparkled with supernatural radiance. She shook her head and squeezed her eyes shut as tightly as she could, hoping to bring back a more plausible vision of reality.

"You're not alone." The flower spoke in a gentle voice as she released a soft mist into the pyramid-shaped tent.

Oona opened one eye. The orchid let out a sigh of relief.

"It's about time!" she exclaimed.

Oona pulled back and retreated into a corner of the tent. Her heart was pounding.

"Mom …" she whispered instinctively, her voice barely audible.

"Don't be afraid, Oona," the majestic flower said reassuringly. "I'm only a messenger."

"What? But … you're a flower and flowers don't talk!"

"Of course, they do. But, only to those who know how to listen," the orchid continued, tilting its corolla.

Oona's shoulders relaxed a little. Suddenly, the wonderful emissary was surrounded by a golden halo. Oona swallowed, then watched open-mouthed as her hands merged with the orchid's sparkling petals.

"But what …"

Oona didn't have the time to finish her sentence before she was engulfed by a tunnel of light that took her breath away.

Chapter V
The Spirit of Earth

Oona found herself surrounded by fish. Were they swimming or flying? For that matter, was *she* swimming or flying? She couldn't say for sure. Astonished, she reached out to touch the iridescent scales of a silver-finned Napoleon fish, but she was going too fast. All at once she found herself inside a bubble that was floating in a lavender sky.

It landed gently among high grasses that stood as tall as Oona, at the feet of two giant lilac-colored squirrels as big as kangaroos. Then it burst with a popping sound. Her eyes wide with wonder, Oona reached out carefully to touch the animals' purple fur. *They're so soft!* The enormous creatures giggled happily and gazed at her affectionately.

The fresh air smelled like spring, wild strawberries, and sunshine. Oona took off her glasses, polished them with her sweatshirt sleeve, and blinked several times.

But … it's a miracle …! She could see perfectly without her glasses. Holding them up to her face, Oona was startled to see her irises reflected in the lenses: no longer just a pale green, now they reflected the continents and oceans of Earth!

"Follow me," a warm breeze whispered in her ear.

She looked up, flabbergasted, and ventured down a path lined with huge, shimmering flowers. Before her was a colossal glass staircase encircled by white, fluffy clouds. An extraordinarily beautiful woman, as huge as the sky, with a kindly face and incredibly long hair appeared above the clouds, illuminating her surroundings with a golden light.

Oona opened her mouth, but no sound came out. She stared at the goddess, unable to move. She was simultaneously frightened and hypnotized by her supernatural beauty. *Was she hallucinating?*

The mysterious woman's huge face leaned toward Oona, her aquamarine eyes radiating unconditional love.

"*Oona, min tolthae …* [*Oona, my child …*]," the goddess greeted her. "I am Eterna, the Spirit of Earth."

Oona was stunned to discover that she could understand her language.

"The Spirit of Earth?" she repeated in disbelief.

Myriads of phosphorescent fish and multicolored birds appeared within Eterna's wavy mane. Then, at the top of the stairs, a crystal door in a glittering palace opened. The goddess reappeared under the arched doorway of a glass pagoda in her human form, wearing a beautiful translucent cape dotted with stars, a white eagle resting on her graceful shoulder. Oona stepped back, dumbstruck.

"There's no need to be afraid, Oona," Eterna said reassuringly.

Oona couldn't take her eyes off the goddess, dazzled by her supernatural beauty.

"Where … where are we?"

"We are on Althaleia, deep in Earth's heart. This is my sanctuary."

A white Persian cat was lounging on the back of a giraffe with plum-colored spots and blue horns, which came over to graze on the grass at Oona's feet. *That looks like the camelopard in Mom's painting*, she thought, mystified. The cat meowed, as if divining her thoughts.

"This is the Kingdom of Life, the cradle of Creation," Eterna proclaimed, her voice full of pride.

A turtle made its way slowly across the luminescent grass, its shell gleaming with pearly geometric patterns. The enormous creature extended its neck toward a beehive buzzing with purple and white bees.

"I summoned you because I need your help, *min tolthae*."

"My … my help?" Oona stammered.

Eterna stared at her with her large eyes and blinked her lime-green lashes.

"Time is short, so I'll tell you the whole Prophecy later. First, I had to test your abilities. You passed with flying colors."

"I did? What test?" Oona asked, wide-eyed.

"Alwilan, whom you named Cosmos, is one of my creations. He has a congenital disorder and can't fly. You saved him from being hit by one of your strange smoke vehicles. You didn't know it but, by rescuing him, you passed your first test."

Oona was speechless.

"You saved his life. Oona, I have great hopes that you can save mine, too. Your heart is ready."

"Are you in danger?"

"Not just me."

A circle topped by a crescent moon started to gleam on Eterna's forehead.

"At the beginning of time, every human was connected to my heart by a filament of light," she explained with a sad smile.

The goddess stretched her arms skyward. An opaque sphere adorned with geometrical patterns appeared before Oona's eyes. The young girl stifled an exclamation of surprise. Next, the wondrous ball became translucent, revealing an enchanting vision of the Earth, a lush paradise where all human beings were connected to Eterna by a luminous thread. Their eyes reflected her continents and oceans, and their faces glowed with happiness.

"Child of the cosmos, I'll die soon, and all humans will perish with me if we don't stop her. We must stop her course!" she exclaimed.

Oona felt a knot in her stomach.

"Stop who?" she whispered, as her mind was flooded all at once by a million questions.

Eterna looked at Oona with infinite sadness.

"Astera, the spirit of the Dark Planet," she explained.

In the middle of the sphere there appeared a woman with glowing hair who was draped in shadows. Despite herself, Oona shivered.

"Astera is jealous of Earth's beauty. She is in love with the Sun, but the Sun loves me. She's extinguishing the stars one by one, feeding off their light to increase her own beauty. But by spreading darkness throughout the cosmos, she is destroying Life! And if she continues her foolish quest, the Sun will be extinguished too, and she will be beautiful but alone, with no one to admire her! She sent Asura, her devoted servant and avatar, to Earth to destroy me."

In the ball, a man in black, shiny armor made of a strange liquid material was kneeling before Astera. The dark liquid molded seamlessly to his face and body, making his features unrecognizable.

"Asura can manifest as a man or as the Dark Cloud, the most terrifying weapon you can imagine. That's what cut the threads of light and severed the connection between humans and my heart," Eterna continued, her voice filled with sadness.

As she spoke, the hologram illustrated her words: a black, oily substance was slowly enveloping the planet in its sinister cloak and gradually infesting the brains of all humans. Their eyes stopped reflecting the terrestrial orb and the sacred filaments of light dissolved in the air. Terrified, Oona breathed in deeply.

"Asura enslaved Earthlings and gathered an army. His soldiers started by contaminating the air they breathe and the water they drink. They've exterminated many animal species, ignoring the supreme web of Life." As Eterna spoke, her voice filled with fury.

Inside the sphere, groups of hunters were capturing dolphins, whales and a herd of elephants, leaving smears of blood in the reddened sky.

Oona reached out to touch the globe. Her throat tightened and tears welled up in her eyes. The ball spun in the air.

"My ice is melting dangerously."

Now the sphere showed a swimming polar bear. Oona could read the worry, then the panic, in the animal's eyes. Eventually, the creature managed to reach a small block of ice floating on the warming waters. Then, it looked around fearfully as the ice floe melted and shrank.

"Noooo!" exclaimed Oona, heartbroken.

"I need your help to restore the filaments of light and free humans from the yoke of the Dark Planet, before it's too late."

Oona swallowed. All the new experiences and new knowledge had left her completely overwhelmed and she felt dizzy.

Eterna looked pointedly at the hologram, which now showed an adolescent girl braving a downpour amidst menacing shadows. Surrounded by crackling flames, the girl valiantly held up a crystal in front of Astera. As she rose into the air, her fearless face became visible: it was Oona! Staring at this dark, distorted image of herself, Oona shuddered at the thought of the confrontation promised by this ominous vision. *And what was this crystal?*

"At the next solar eclipse, you'll have to confront Astera."

"That can't be me!"

"It most certainly is. However, Oona, you are free to decline this mission and return to Earth if you wish," Eterna said in a soft voice.

Oona felt feverish.

"I'm sorry but all this is too much … It's just … I've got to get back to school … and I can't leave my mother alone. Do you understand?" Oona pleaded, panicking.

"Your heart has made it possible for you to travel through space and time. You would only be gone for the earthly equivalent of a few moments, a day or two at most. It's your destiny, *min tolthae*."

Oona shook her head. She had in fact felt alone and different for as long as she could remember. As she gazed at Eterna at the top of the crystal stairs, her thoughts were racing uncontrollably. The orchid bent her flowering stems toward her and seemed to be waiting for an answer. Oona's vision started to blur, but she didn't know if it was from near-sightedness or shock.

"I … I can't! I'm sorry but I really can't!" Oona protested, hating herself for disappointing the benevolent goddess.

"As you wish, *min tolthae*," Eterna replied, smiling softly.

Then Oona heard a deafening *whoosh* as first her hair and then her entire body was sucked into a powerful current of hot air.

CHAPTER VI
Despair

When Oona opened her eyes again, she gasped in surprise. She was back in her regular spot at the back of the bus, with Cosmos chirping loudly in her lap. She blinked under the weight of her glasses and realized she was near-sighted again. She sighed. *Why had Eterna sent her back to Earth on the school bus?* Daylight was already fading as the vehicle approached the reservation, meaning she must have missed a day of school and be on her way home now. *What had happened to her? What will happen to Eterna now?! To … everyone on Earth?* As she caught sight of the Chumash forest, Oona unconsciously sat up straight in her seat, then removed her glasses and tried to make out her reflection in the lenses. Despite her concerns, she tried to fix her hair, suddenly conscious of how asymmetrical the cut was, then watched the road. Her heart started to beat a strange rhythm. *Would the cute boy be there?* Her thoughts shot uncontrollably through her mind like bolts of lightning! *Ridiculous*, she scolded herself, shaking her head and putting her glasses back on. As if she didn't have better things to think about, what with her mother's condition and the threat the Earth was facing! Abruptly, the bus made a ninety-degree turn and went inland. She felt Cosmos clutching her skin with his little talons to keep from falling onto the floor.

"Kids, we've got to go a different route because they're cutting down the trees on the reservation," Mrs. Daniels announced into the microphone.

Oona's jaw dropped. She opened her window and, stretching her neck out as far as she could, until it felt like she might fall out, she turned her head toward the rear end of the bus. That's when she saw him. Her stomach dropped as if she were on a roller coaster and a surprised giggle escaped her lips. The boy was waving a sign and standing next to a tiny old lady with a feathered headdress that reminded Oona of a peacock, along with about a dozen other Chumash people wearing their traditional regalia.

The signs read: "No to deforestation! Respect nature, respect life!"

In front of them, chainsaws were cutting into the massive trunks of majestic trees, making a deafening roar as they sent shards of pale wood flying into the air. Frantically, Oona covered her ears. The noise of the chainsaws contrasted dramatically with the silence of their victims. The noble trees stood tall and seemed to maintain their dignity in front of their executioners. With much squawking and rustling of wings, birds were fleeing their nests. They were going to have to find new homes! From afar, Oona witnessed the magnificent sequoias falling to the ground one after the other, their branches seeming to beseech the heavens like arms lifted in a cry for help. Then their foliage, golden and radiant with life, shivered one last time before losing its luster. The sap flowed down their trunks like the tears coursing down Oona's cheeks. Sadness welled up in her throat. She opened her mouth to shout "No!" at the barbarians who were killing these innocent beings and assailing the Spirit of the Earth, but no sound emerged.

"Eterna …" she murmured, sitting back down and lowering her eyes.

Should she have agreed to help her? she wondered, nervously stroking the top of Cosmos's head. The question spun around in her head like a windmill, and she felt crushed by an overwhelming sense of guilt.

When she looked up again, the bus was slowing down as it approached her home. In the distance, she could see the silhouette of two men on the front steps but couldn't make out who they were. She started to get a bad feeling and kept peering at the strangers.

The bus had barely come to a stop when Oona jumped up, hid Cosmos in her sweatshirt, and ran toward home. The sound of a siren assaulted her eardrums as the blue and red lights of an ambulance flashed across the front of the house before driving away. Anxiety surged through Oona. "Mommy!" she whispered, trembling.

Her father appeared in the doorway with a snide look on his face. Oona saw his cold eyes light up with satisfaction and she shivered in fear.

Where were they taking her mother? Her blood froze with terror. She couldn't live alone with her father, it was out of the question! Her stomach churned and she felt as if she were falling into a bottomless pit. Cosmos chirped, then screeched at the top of his lungs and flapped his wings against her chest as if to bring her back to life. Oona gasped for air and held the baby bird close to her. Glancing at her father's hands, she noticed they were black with soot. Or was it grease? Had he been working on a car engine? She frowned. That was an unlikely scenario. And what were those pools of black ink on the front steps? She was suffocating. In a panic, she turned and ran toward the ocean.

Chapter VII
Come Back, Cosmos!

Once on the beach, Oona stopped and surveyed the horizon, panting. Looking around, she observed an epic sight that did not bode well: a huge traffic jam of cars seemed to be trying to leave all at once. Oona tightened her grip on Cosmos's fragile body and accosted a man who was racing past her. "Excuse me, sir, what's going on?!"

"It's the ocean … the tide suddenly went out, and look! The whole sky is turning black!" he answered hastily, then turned to rush away.

All at once, it seemed to her that the ground was shaking, as the sand moved all around her. She shuddered as she thought of the melting ice cap and the poor polar bear clinging desperately to its block of ice. She almost screamed, "Eterna!"

"Run! Find your parents as soon as you can!" the man urged, looking dazed.

Oona took a deep breath of salty air, turned around, and started to run back home. She almost tripped on the seaweed the powerful ocean wind had strewn across the sand. This seemingly never-ending day had left her exhausted and she could barely stay on her feet. When she reached home, Oona noticed that her father's car was gone. *Of course! Why would he wait for her if a storm was threatening to hit the coast? Better off seeking shelter inland*, she thought, shaking her head in disbelief. Her throat tightened as a scene from the past flashed before her eyes. One day he'd taken her skiing, overriding her mother's objections that the weather was taking an ominous turn. She was four or five years old at the time, with a new red parka and two smooth pigtails. As soon as they'd reached the top of the mountain, the blizzard set in. Her father had shot off down a black diamond ski slope, leaving her standing there alone, a forlorn crimson dot amid the swirling flakes. The mountain patrollers had found her and brought her back home to her mother, who was on the verge of a nervous breakdown. That day, Oona had felt fear like she never had known before. *Was it possible that he wasn't actually her father?!*

She shook her head to chase away the bitter memories, ran to her room, and rushed to the window to watch the sea. Cosmos slipped out of her arms and fell straight to the ground like a bundle of feathers. Then, panic-stricken, he fluttered around on the floor.

"Cosmos!" she shouted.

There was a dull, menacing roar. Through the window, Oona saw the ocean rising relentlessly toward them below strange columns of black smoke. What mysterious clouds! She picked Cosmos up and he buried his head in her armpit as a tremendous blast shattered the windowpane. The blast of salty air threw Oona violently backwards As she crashed against the wall, she accidentally let go of the little bird. He looked at her beseechingly but … it was too late! In a split second, the little creature was picked up by the wind, drawn out the window and carried out to sea.

"Cosmos!!!"

That was the last thing Oona remembered seeing before losing consciousness. A few moments later, when she woke up, an enormous wave was receding in the distance and several stars were lighting up the evening sky.

"Cosmos!" she called out in despair, over and over again as she stared miserably at the orange horizon.

Stricken with grief, she collapsed to the debris-covered floor, and hid her head in her hands, shaking with sobs.

Once her crying subsided, she lay motionless on the floor for what seemed like an eternity. Her nose was running, and strands of hair stuck to her tear-stained face. Eventually, Oona raised her head and looked at the white orchid, lying on its side among the torn books and scattered objects, miraculously spared, and then at her star twinkling in the reddish sky. What was she doing on planet Earth? She no longer had a family. Actually, she'd never had one! All her friends and acquaintances had at least one parent, protector, or guide. All at once, she felt overwhelmingly alone, so tiny, so lost, with no place in the human world where she belonged. She was well aware that her brain didn't work like other people's did, that she had an unusual way of looking at things. Only animals seemed to understand her. And she was irresistibly attracted to what lay beyond the world, to the stars.

Filled with a newfound sense of purpose, Oona stood up and grabbed the flower.

"Miss … Flower, I must speak to Eterna!"

Nothing happened. She repeated her summons, raising her voice. "I beg you, I must speak to Eterna … as soon as possible!" she added, trembling.

Suddenly, a blinding white light filled her vision, and her heart was filled with a comforting warmth.

CHAPTER VIII
The Guardians of Earth

When she opened her eyes again, she was floating amid fluffy clouds, which formed and reformed in an amazing variety of shapes: a lion, a swan and, finally, the almighty Eterna, beautiful as ever, with hair now made of iridescent butterflies. Little by little the light subsided, revealing emerald-green valleys covered with multicolored hibiscus, watered by a turquoise lagoon. Oona's lungs were filled with crisp air, as if she were on the summit of a very high mountain. The delicate scent of jasmine and cinnamon perfumed the air.

"Your Majesty … Eterna," she stammered. "I made a mistake. I … I lost Cosmos! I'm very sorry." She took off her glasses, which were of no use now on Althaleia and made a gesture of respect. "Tell me what I need to do, I beg you …" she implored, kneeling awkwardly before the celestial goddess, her face lifted toward her.

Eterna was smiling at her lovingly. Suddenly, two bubbles appeared in the immaculate sky and landed on the smooth grass next to Oona. Inside each bubble floated a young person. Her eyes widened in surprise as she recognized the Chumash boy. The continents of the Earth were reflected in his chestnut-colored eyes. Despite herself, a shiver of joy ran through her body. For a moment, she even forgot about losing Cosmos!

"My child, how wonderful it is to see you again!" exclaimed Eterna, bowing her head toward Oona, her eyes sparkling.

Dolphins were jumping in her hair and bursting into laughter, as if to express her joy. Oona giggled despite herself.

"Thank you for coming to help me. Don't worry, you won't be alone on your quest. Oona, I'd like to introduce you to the other Guardians of Earth," the goddess announced ceremoniously. "They've been looking forward to your arrival."

They were looking forward to her arrival? The second bubble contained an elegant young girl, perhaps twelve or thirteen years old, with very dark skin and a proud bearing. In her jade-colored irises Oona could also see the continents of the Earth.

"I am Nawal, the Guardian of the Waters. From Malakal, near Lake No in Sudan. My ancestors are Sumerian and Aksumite," the young girl said calmly.

Oona nodded her head in greeting.

"I am Aqiwo, the Guardian of the Forests. From California. My ancestors are Chumash," the boy said in turn.

Aqiwo, Oona said to herself, savoring the sound of it. Her heart started beating in the same irregular way it had when she'd been on the bus.

"Hello. I'm Oona … I'm not sure who my ancestors are," she added shyly.

Nawal and Aqiwo bowed their heads, as if they already knew her origins.

"*Min tolthi* – my children, we haven't got much time left," Eterna declared, her face pale as snow. "My forests are burning, my oceans are raging …" the goddess continued, heartbroken. "I am growing ever weaker," she murmured, her eyes brimming with tears. "The Earth is becoming more and more ravaged every day. Soon I will die, the humans with me. They don't understand that their plight is connected to my destiny," she sighed. "You must find the Supreme Crystal before the next solar eclipse. It gives omniscience to whoever possesses it. Only the Supreme Crystal will enable you to restore the threads of light that joined me to human hearts, so harmony with Nature can reign again and I'll be spared."

"Venerable Eterna, how should we go about finding the Supreme Crystal?" Aqiwo inquired uneasily.

"Your quest will be fraught with danger. First, you will need to find Three Keys."

"Three Keys?" Oona queried.

"Yes, the Luminous Beings have written clues on the skin of your arms," the goddess replied. "Each clue will lead you to a key, and, once united, the Three Keys will lead you to the Supreme Crystal. You must solve each of the three riddles and find the crystal before Astera does. May the clues appear now!" Eterna proclaimed, shaking her hair, now made of seaweed.

The three young people watched wide-eyed as mysterious patterns appeared on their forearms. Oona ran her fingers in disbelief over the new gold markings on her skin: a brilliant triangle next to three dots surrounded by radiating beams of light like shooting stars. She looked at Nawal and Aqiwo to see what kind of markings were now inscribed on their arms. Noticing her curiosity, Aqiwo gave her a knowing look. Embarrassed, she immediately lowered her eyes and hid behind her hair.

"Who are the Luminous Beings?" asked Nawal, amazed.

"Let me tell you their story," Eterna began. "The Luminous Beings were far more advanced than humans. These selfless beings had mastered the power of light and were the only species in the cosmos capable of creating new stars in the sky."

"They have the power to create stars?" Oona whispered, stunned.

"They *had* the power. For now they are no longer," said Eterna, her voice trembling. "When the Luminous Beings found out about Astera's sinister plan, they decided to sacrifice their star, the brightest one in the cosmos, to infuse a crystal with its light and save me. That is the Supreme Crystal."

Oona hung on the goddess's every word, her heart aching with grief as she thought of these kind aliens.

"They're … dead?" murmured Oona.

Eterna nodded. Oona's heart sank.

"And … Why us?" Aqiwo asked.

"The Luminous Beings hid the Supreme Crystal on Earth in such a way as to ensure that only those with a pure heart could find it," Eterna told them, placing her flower-covered hand over her verdant heart. "Each of you has passed the test. Your powers will be revealed in due time."

Powers … Like supernatural powers? Oona stifled a gasp of astonishment. Picturing herself flying over the ocean, she couldn't help but smile.

"I now entrust you to the care of Master Wada and Thothan, my eagle, who will teach you the Lessons of Life," Eterna added mysteriously. "For the Prophecy tells that you will confront both Astera and Asura in the course of this quest. For you to do so and emerge victorious, you must learn how to fight!"

Oona felt knots of apprehension form in her belly.

CHAPTER IX
Lesson Number One

Eterna disappeared through the door of the glass pagoda and re-emerged above her palace, glorious in her ethereal form. Spellbound, Oona clasped her hands to her chest. Then, the bubbles formed again around each child, this time including Oona, who gazed in amazement at the translucent material, shaped like a perfect sphere, that surrounded her. She carefully touched the wall, which molded itself around her index and covered it with multicolored sparkles. Eterna's long hair began to flutter, and a wave crashed loudly at her feet, the resulting bubbles carried off in the ocean of her aquamarine curls. Oona squealed in surprise, then giggled happily as her own bubble rolled into the turquoise waves.

The white eagle followed them into the stream of Eterna's blue hair. Oona could feel her heart thudding in her chest as she contemplated the liquid surrounding her on all sides. Then, the curtain of water parted before her eyes to reveal enormous mountains that looked like the Himalayas except for one tiny difference: these mountains were floating in the air, suspended like clouds of emerald foam in an infinite sky. The three bubbles gave a little pop as they burst and released the Guardians in the middle of a lush rainforest bordered by towering cliffs. Oona gazed openmouthed at her surroundings, captivated by their beauty. Eterna's glass pagoda glittered from where it was encircled by blossoming cherry trees, the tiered roof resembling an enormous jewel.

The eagle flew toward the top of the stairs and vanished behind a massive pillar. Something drove a huge furry macaque out of the bushes and it ran away, yelping. Oona let out a gasp. A dense fog fell over the translucent pagoda and the eagle reappeared at the top of the crystal stairs, then transformed into a graceful human being with a shimmering baby chick on his head. Oona's eyes widened as the tiny creature fluttered about, leaving glittering trails in the air.

"Cosmos! You're alive!!" she cried, rushing toward him.

Cosmos chirped jubilantly and flapped his wings, as though trying to fly toward her. Stunned, Oona stared at him through tears of joy.

"Honorable Guardian, I am Thothan," the birdman said, by way of reply. "But some call me Snow Arrow.

Alwilan, or shall I say Cosmos, is my son. I thank you for saving him."

"But I didn't manage to save him … I thought he'd been carried away by the storm!" she said, with a catch in her voice.

"It was all orchestrated by Althaleia, my child. You did in fact spare him from a fatal collision with one of your four-wheeled monsters. Since he was unable to fly on his own, the Wind brought him back home to us."

Oona gazed at Cosmos, speechless.

"Can I …?" she stammered.

Thothan nodded his head in consent and Oona reached out to stroke the little bird's downy feathers, sensing that the tiny creature's heart was exploding with joy. He burrowed his head in the hollow of her hand and gave her gentle, affectionate taps with his beak.

"Alwilan …" she murmured, her eyes filling with happy tears.

Although her mother's absence was a constant pain in her heart, at least she and Cosmos were reunited.

The sound of a gong interrupted their reunion. Behind Thothan stood a tiny, wrinkled woman in a kimono, holding an enormous mallet in front of a golden disc several yards wide that was suspended from a hook in the ceiling like a moon in the sky. How could that little body have the strength to hold such a big mallet at arm's length? She glided back and forth in front the young people as if she were rolling on wheels over the floor. She struck the instrument again cheerfully, and Oona jumped and stumbled over a root. Delighted by Oona's reaction, the old woman let out a high-pitched laugh. *What a strange sense of humor!* Oona thought, perplexed.

"This is the Venerable Elder, Master Wada," sighed the half-human, half-eagle being. He frowned in an apparent effort to remain impassive. "Master Wada is a Bhuddist nun who teaches kung fu. As for me, I'm Eterna's messenger to the animals and the elements – water, air, fire, and earth," he announced proudly.

"Welcome to the Kingdom of Eterna!" the woman in the kimono exclaimed with a broad smile. "Eterna is the source of all power. Her beauty and omniscience are everywhere, maintaining the harmony of the cosmos. As my dear friend Thothan told you, I am Master Wada, your new kung fu teacher. Kung fu is a form of meditation that gives access to cosmic power."

"Aqiwo and Nawal have already spent two blue moons here, or approximately two hundred and twenty-eight Earth days, learning how to fight" Thothan said, nodding toward her companions.

Oona turned around and saw Aqiwo and Nawal defending themselves with martial arts sticks. Dressed in a pastel kimono, Nawal was gracefully fighting a kind of snake with little pink wings while dodging fireballs thrown at her by a creature that looked a lot like a panda.

"We have very little time, so you must try to catch up with them," urged Master Wada. "Eterna is getting weaker every day and you need to become strong if you're going to fight Astera."

How would she be able to keep up with her companions? She'd never manage it! They were almost a year ahead of her and she only had a few days to catch up with them. Plus, she didn't really like kung fu to begin with. Unless, that is, martial arts were a means of controlling one's mind and achieving self-mastery, she thought, remembering the Chinese legend of Hua Mulan.

"Master Wada, Venerable Thothan, I don't know if I'll be able to do it!"

Master Wada patted her on the top of her head and laughed. Oona hunched her shoulders, decidedly unreceptive to the nun's sense of humor.

"Doubting yourself is forbidden. Understood?"

"Be confident," added the eagle. "Eterna will be by your side, and we will show you the secrets of her power."

"Give it back!" Aqiwo shouted, in a tone at once forceful and imploring.

Oona's looked up. The boy was standing on a branch high in a tree, confronting a monkey that was holding a rectangular wooden object it had apparently stolen. From afar, it looked like a little painting. Aqiwo was about to fall but, with amazing agility, managed to grab a vine and tear the object from the grimacing primate's hairy hands. The flexible stem wrapped itself around the trunk and brought him to the ground. With a sigh of relief, he clutched the precious item to his chest. Although she didn't understand its significance, Oona couldn't help but be happy for him.

"Copy my movements and I'll teach you the foundations of Shaolin kung fu," Master Wada said to her.

Oona's stomach knotted with fear. She *had* to impress them … no matter what! Taking a deep breath of fresh jasmine-scented air to calm herself down, she followed instructions, copying the Master's movements. Then the Venerable Elder reached out for a jade ball the size of a watermelon that was sitting atop a moss-covered stone colonnade. The huge ball lifted into the air and darted toward Oona. She shrieked and fell backwards, barely dodging the heavy missile. Disappointed at her lack of reflexes, she shook her head, ashamed. How did Master Wada manage to get such a heavy ball to fly? The nun shrieked with laughter again. Oona looked at her, astounded.

"But … How did you do it?"

"Later, later," Master Wada replied cheerfully. "It's through the power of Eterna. The first part of this Lesson is over. Follow me," she continued. "Now I'll teach you to control your emotions." She pointed to a transparent wall with an egg-shaped alcove, barely taller than Oona, carved into it.

"Stand up straight in front of the wall," the Venerable Elder ordered as she glided away.

Obediently, Oona positioned herself against the wall.

"Now, no matter what happens, don't move," Master Wada ordered.

Oona frowned. She straightened up and threw her shoulders back to give herself courage.

"No matter what happens?" she asked.

Her legs faltered.

"Don't ask questions. Just don't move. Understand?" interjected Thothan, who was standing about ten yards away from Oona.

Oona nodded as her palms grew damp with apprehension.

"And keep your eyes open," the old woman continued. "Thothan, are you ready? Go ahead."

The eagle, now in his human form, threw two ice daggers at her. Oona's eyes widened and her heart almost stopped as she saw the blades flying straight toward her.

Letting out a cry and closing her eyes, she threw herself backwards against the wall. CLANG! The knives hit the wall, grazing her burning ears before shattering. She slowly opened her eyes again, legs trembling.

"I said to keep your eyes open," the sage scolded. "And your mouth closed. You must learn to control your fear and your body. Focus your eyes on the tree behind me. Breathe slowly," she commanded as Thothan threw two more daggers at her.

Oona focused on the blue cypress tree behind her and forced herself to keep her eyes open. Her jaw clenched and as her entire body tensed, she pushed against the wall behind her as if to *disappear* inside the egg-shaped alcove.

"That's better. If you master your fear, only your power remains, because fear and power cannot coexist. Controlling your emotions is the subject of the first Lesson," Master Wada said, her bright eyes twinkling.

Now Thothan started bombarding her with ice knives. Oona tried to remain still, but her legs trembled uncontrollably, betraying her fear.

The Venerable Elder continued her litany in a low, hypnotic voice.

"Calm your mind. Listen to Eterna."

Oona breathed deeply and closed her eyes. Her mind became clear. The sounds faded and all she could hear were the rustling sounds of Master Wada's fluid movements. Whooosh, the icy blades hissed. When she opened her eyes again, she saw that the Master was standing next to Thothan in attack position. Perched on his father's head, Cosmos was shielding his eyes with his tiny wings. Oona could sense the baby bird's concern for her as the kimono-clad nun challenged her to a duel. Her pulse quickened and her cheeks flushed.

"Listen to nature, the animals, the elements. They are your guides," Master Wada told her in a melodious voice, bearing down on Oona in a flash.

"This way …" the wind whispered in her ears.

Oona obeyed, just barely avoiding the old woman's fist.

"Watch out for her feet," whispered the flowers.

A leopard with reddish-pink spots growled. "Jump now!" the feline advised.

Oona abandoned her body to the murmurs of the mountains, which encouraged her to counter the Master's offensive by using her flexibility. She managed to dodge most of the attacks by quickly swaying her body, like a reed bending in the wind.

Oona found herself making rapid progress over the course of the next few hours, managing to master such feats as doing cartwheels while suspended over the flames of an emerald-colored fire. Then, to escape the menacing flames, she used both hands to grab suspension bars that were floating in midair. Finally, she climbed onto a pair of bamboo stilts and ran over multicolored snakes.

"Your accelerated training has been most fruitful," Thothan assured her. Oona's chest filled with joy. She hadn't felt such happiness in a long time.

"Daughter of the cosmos, Eterna wilts. It is time for your final initiation," continued the eagle, still in his human form, his tone marked by the utmost gravity.

"My final initiation?" asked Oona, gasping for breath. This did not bode well. Especially since Master Wada was again doubled over with laughter.

CHAPTER X
Lesson Number Two

Thothan gestured for the three youngsters to fall in behind him as he followed Master Wada, who was leading the way. They took a winding path through the flower-filled canyon and began to climb the side of a mountain. The sharp drop at the edge of the path made Oona lightheaded and her vision blurred. The gorge was filled with a sea of clouds and there was a breathtaking view of another mountain floating in the distance. Master Wada suddenly materialized on the other side of the dizzyingly steep ravine.

"I'm waiting for you!" the nun shouted, her voice echoing from all directions.

"What are we supposed to do?" exclaimed Oona, furtively glancing at Aqiwo.

She'd been hoping that his face would show the same amazement that she was feeling, but nothing of the kind! He must have got used to Master Wada's outlandish requests during his previous training with her. Nawal just shot her a cold look.

"Control your mind. Imagine yourself next to Master Wada. Your body will follow," explained Thothan, who had stayed with the apprentice Guardians. Still perched on top of his head, Alwilan gave a shrill whistle of approval.

Aqiwo stepped forward, the wind blowing his silky black hair.

"Are you saying that we must jump? But that's crazy!" exclaimed Oona, aghast.

The young boy winked at his new companions, breathed in deeply, then threw himself into the void. Oona put her hand over her mouth to keep from screaming. Aqiwo flew gracefully through Althaleia's skies, but suddenly a gust of wind sprang up and pushed him violently backwards. He dropped suddenly, like a marionette abandoned by its puppeteer. Oona looked away, her blood pounding in her temples. Aqiwo, however, seemed undeterred. Visibly exerting himself, he managed to regain the height he had lost and, after a true feat of strength, he reached the mountain top. Panting, he turned around and waved to Oona and Nawal from the other side, his right hand on his chest. Oona let out a sigh. She was relieved Aqiwo wasn't standing next to her, as her flushed cheeks would doubtless have betrayed her feelings.

"Aqiwo, you've made progress, but your doubts are still getting in the way," Master Wada said, her voice echoing indistinctly across the ravine.

Meanwhile, Nawal was standing next to Oona, ignoring her encouraging smiles. Worse, Oona had the distinct impression that she was trying to avoid her gaze. *Had she inadvertently said or done something to offend her?* Oona drove this unpleasant thought from her mind as she watched the other girl approach the abyss. Nawal closed her eyes, then threw herself into the void without the slightest hesitation, making a swan dive toward the floating mountain. With a smile on her lips, she shot through the air like a missile and landed gracefully near Aqiwo with disconcerting ease.

As Oona drew close to the edge of the precipice, she was enveloped by a swarm of cyan-colored dragonflies with striped, wasp-like bodies.

"What are these?" she yelled, leaping backwards.

"Royal dragonflies," shouted Thothan from the other side of the canyon.

"And here I thought there were no bugs in heaven!" blurted Nawal, who seemed to be terrified of insects.

"We aren't in paradise, Nawal, but on Althaleia," the eagle reminded her as he watched Oona approach the void.

Her vision eclipsed by a hazy fog, Oona pulled back.

"Have faith in yourself," Master Wada called, cupping her hands around her mouth to create a kind of megaphone.

"I'm scared of heights!" Oona replied as she tottered on wobbly legs, despising herself for her weakness.

"Listen to the air. Eterna is always near you," Thothan assured her.

"I'm listening but I don't hear anything!"

Oona gazed at the sky. She thought she could see a swan on a blanket of purplish clouds.

"Eterna?" she called, questioningly.

If somebody had told her the day before that she'd be talking to clouds … She glanced at her two companions waiting for her on the other side. She had to be confident, and then her body would follow. Yet another adage that was easy enough to say but hard to follow.

Gathering her courage, Oona jumped forward. And immediately began to fall. Screaming as if her final moment had come, she disappeared into a blanket of clouds. Thothan's booming voice reached her through the sound of Alwilan's panicked chirping.

"Breathe and focus," he counseled.

Oona breathed deeply to focus her mind, but abruptly stopped her intake of breath when she felt feathers tickling her body. She reappeared above the white fluffy mantle, sporting long wings formed by a flock of blue jays that brought her back to the edge of the canyon.

Frustrated by her failure, she opened her mouth to apologize, but the eagle silenced her with a wave of his hand. He shook his head.

"At least you jumped. Your heart is brave and you have faith in Eterna."

Eterna's immense face filled the sky, wilted daffodils falling from her glorious hair. All-powerful, she proclaimed, "The time has come for you to believe in yourself."

"I know I can do it," Oona exclaimed, frowning. She was determined to pass this test.

"Perhaps, deep down, you don't actually believe it," the goddess suggested.

Eterna's forehead started to glow, and the sphere she had seen before, now topped with a crescent moon, materialized before Oona's eyes. Inside, she could see her father. His sometimes-cutting words echoed in her head and she shrank back.

"The minds of some humans are enshrouded by the Dark Cloud and this creates an abyss in their hearts. Forget their hurtful or discouraging words. You did nothing wrong."

Oona walked reluctantly to the edge of the cliff, her vision blurring a little more with each step. It was then that she felt something quivering against her neck. Alwilan was fluttering around next to her face and brushing her cheek with his wing.

"Alwilan?" she asked in astonishment as the chick planted himself in front of her and flapped his wings frantically above the void. "But … But you can fly!"

The tiny creature let out a little shriek of delight and did pirouettes in the air. She couldn't believe her eyes! Thrilled, Oona clasped her hands together as if to applaud.

"You see, your love has given him wings," Eterna murmured tenderly.

The little bird nodded as if in agreement. Moved by a burst of enthusiasm, Oona took a deep breath and leapt bravely into the void. The wispy haze of the clouds passed before her eyes as she fell or flew straight ahead, she couldn't tell which. Inside her cloudy cocoon, an infinite silence prevailed. After a moment that seemed like an eternity, a patch of blue sky tore through the fluffy mass of clouds. She felt like she was supported by an invisible bridge, gliding effortlessly to the peak of the other floating mountain.

"You did it!" Aqiwo shouted, arms raised in victory.

Heartened by the other Guardian's words, Oona felt a wave of contentment wash over her. Aqiwo's eyes glowed as he looked at her. She looked away, smiling shyly.

"The Power is in you," said Master Wada, crinkling her eyes. "That's the purpose of the second Lesson."

"Never forget it. It's one of the most important lessons," Thothan announced.

"Along with the recipe for fennel rice!" chuckled the old woman.

This time, Oona laughed. Nawal and Aqiwo, on the other hand, looked at the old woman, perplexed.

"Follow me," Thothan exhorted. "Your trials have only just begun."

Eterna's long, silky hair began to wave around them, revealing myriads of flowers and birds, rainbow-colored animals, and all kinds of colorful creatures that made up the flora and fauna of Althaleia. Suddenly, Oona let out a long, high-pitched wail and Thothan stopped abruptly. She was emitting a strange melody.

"The song of the whales!" he exclaimed.

"What's going on? What's happening to me?" asked Oona, shocked.

"The whales are using you to communicate with us. This means that your powers are starting to reveal themselves," Eterna observed. "And that it won't be long before it's clear what Nawal's and Aqiwo's are as well."

"Whales are capable of communicating across great distances by using special, unique frequencies," Nawal said in an expressionless voice. "They are more effective than sonar and can replicate human language. But wait a second. How do I know all this?" she continued, bewildered.

"You've been granted the gift of knowledge, Nawal," the goddess declared.

"Whales are the only ones that can intercept the thoughts of the Dark Planet!" the eagle exclaimed. "Oona, what message was delivered to you?"

She closed her eyes and focused.

"The whales are in danger. They're … they're coming," she gasped.

What does it mean, 'They're coming'? Where are they coming from? Oona wondered, taken aback. Eterna's hair started to wave violently and several columns of white foam were blown into the air with a deafening whoosh. A pod of humpback whales appeared in the blue light of her swirling hair, their leader clad in a what looked like a ceremonial robe embroidered with seaweed. Oona's eyes widened. Two whale calves appeared at her feet, whimpering. An orca with white spots swam in their direction and, with a father's care, took them in his gargantuan jaws. He seemed to be reprimanding them as he pointed his flipper at the whale in ceremonial costume.

"It's their father!" exclaimed Oona, her eyes wide. "He told them not to disturb their mother while she's working. She's the leader of the whales!"

Turning her huge, bluish head toward Oona, the whale's Leader emitted an anguished cry.

"She says that the Dark Planet has returned! The whales have picked up Astera's thoughts. They're telling me that she's on her way to Giza, in Egypt."

The marine mammals tirelessly relayed the same message over and over, like a melodious underwater lamentation, as a pattern formed in the strands of Eterna's hair, which now had the consistency of sand. Nawal studied the pattern.

"They look like pyramids!" Nawal exclaimed.

Oona covered her ears with her hands, as if to protect her eardrums.

"The Leader says that Astera has also detected the whales' vibrations" she sputtered. "She's sworn to destroy them! The leader of the whales is asking for our help, or else all the whales will die!"

"What should we do?" asked Aqiwo, panicked. As one, they all turned toward Thothan.

"Your priority is to find the Three Keys. I've taught you to listen to Eterna, whose strength will guide you on the right path."

His instructions were concise, to say the least. A wave of trepidation washed over Oona. The task that awaited them seemed enormous. She contemplated the two equilateral triangles inscribed on her forearm.

"What if the triangles are the pyramids? That would mean the First Key is in the pyramids of Giza, right?" she asked her companions, suddenly excited at the thought of having made a discovery.

"I agree, let's go! Besides, we don't really have another choice," replied Aqiwo.

"Join hands," commanded Thothan, resuming his eagle shape. "Your bubbles will form again as soon as your fingers touch. Remember, your heart is your compass."

Master Wada got a running start, then jumped onto the luminous creature's neck.

"And don't forget, it's easy to catch a baby tiger. All you have to do is enter its den!" shouted the sage, digging her hands into the bird's silky plumage.

Oona frowned as she struggled to understand the Venerable Elder's words. Alwilan chirped in Oona's direction as if in farewell while the gigantic bird rose into the sky in a rainbow of sparks, his offspring beneath his wing.

"Alwilan, take care of yourself. I'll miss you!"

The chick peeped tirelessly in response. After some time, all she could see was a white eagle flying in the distance. She gazed at the horizon with a heavy heart.

"Give me your hands and focus," ordered Aqiwo.

The trio sat down in the lotus position and stretched out their hands. Oona felt her heart race as Aqiwo grabbed hers, and her palm tingled where their skin touched.

The Leader of the whales opened her jaw with its thousands of teeth and let out a melodious whistle. Oona nodded her head in agreement.

"The whales will keep us informed," she explained.

The huge marine mammals dove back into Eterna's flowing hair spouting pillars of foam. An electric wave created a blue current among the three Guardians. Oona closed her eyes.

CHAPTER XI
The Pyramids of Giza

When Oona opened her eyes again, she was floating alongside her companions in her bubble over the Sahara Desert. She giggled. Despite the gravity of her mission, she found it hard to feel anything except euphoria as she contemplated the Earth from so high up in her translucent sphere. It was as if she were being held aloft by a soft mattress of warm air that allowed her to turn in all directions. Oona gazed in awe at the golden ocean below her that stretched into the distance. The disc of the rising sun crowned the stately minarets and skyscrapers of the distant city of Cairo. Her bubble dipped and glided over the winding alleys of a nearby village that teemed with life: people in brightly-colored jellabiyas were bartering in the market and ragged, barefoot children were running and juggling lemons. What a contrast to the deserted streets of Los Angeles where nobody got out of their cars!

The Guardians were sailing above the clouds when their bubbles abruptly dropped down into the middle of the desert. For a few seconds Oona panicked, trying in vain to cling to the cushion of air surrounding her body. Above them hovered a shadowy expanse of menacing clouds that streaked the sky red in its wake. The black mass spun around, emitting dark plumes of smoke, before transforming into a face with glowing eyes of lava. Terrified, Oona gulped. Fear chilled her blood. Suddenly, the ominous apparition vanished into the immaculate blue sky.

Her bubble slowed down as it neared the ground, then opened gently like the petals of a flower before depositing her on the burning sand. For a moment, Aqiwo's bubble remained suspended in the sky as if paralyzed by a supernatural force, then burst in midair and dropped the boy onto the crest of a glittering dune.

"We can't go any further," Aqiwo shouted, dusting himself off. He surveyed his surroundings, then ran down the dune. "But what was that weird cloud?"

"Yes, it looked like it had eyes!" exclaimed Nawal, herself wide-eyed. Her whole body trembled as she remained crouched in her bubble, which had just landed near them.

"Eterna told me that Asura could transform into a Dark Cloud," Oona added. "Maybe that's what it was?"

"And the whales warned us that Astera had sent Asura to Giza …" Nawal chimed in tentatively. "But then why didn't he attack us?"

Oona looked at the pattern on her forearm.

"Maybe Asura doesn't know where the Three Keys are. He needs us," she ventured, running her fingers over the gold tattoos on her skin.

"We don't have any time to lose, then! Let's make our way to the pyramids!" exclaimed Aqiwo breathlessly.

"I think the wind brought us near the city of Tanis," advised Oona, recalling something she'd read in one of her books on the pyramids. "We have to get closer to the city of Cairo and then we'll probably have to walk to Giza," she said, as her bubble vanished in a shower of sparks.

Surrounded by ocher-colored dunes, it was as if they were in the middle of a sea of sand that had been frozen in time.

"But which way should we go?" asked Aqiwo.

Feeling a warm breeze all around her, Oona closed her eyes to listen to the elements tell her their secrets, just as Thothan had taught her. The air caressed her cheeks, whispering a melody that sounded like a symphony of panpipes in her ears, then blew through her hair, pushing it toward the west. After a few moments, she pointed her finger resolutely toward the sun.

"The path of the sun," Nawal murmured.

The Guardians climbed the dune in the direction of the shining star closest to the Earth, each of their steps sinking softly into the sparkling sand as they made their way toward the Egyptian capital. After only a short while, Oona began to feel overwhelmed by the absolute silence of the desert.

"Nawal, does Sudan look like Egypt?" she asked, having some difficulty getting the words out because her mouth was parched with thirst.

She was curious to know more about the country that Nawal came from and was secretly hoping to break the ice between them.

"My country was known for its lush vegetation," she replied, her voice cold. "But our rivers and lakes have gone dry. There's no water anymore," the girl sighed, stumbling behind Aqiwo.

"Water …" he said, wiping his sweaty forehead. "We need to find water."

"But how do you survive without water?" Oona persisted, eager to make sense of the distance the other girl seemed intent on keeping between them.

Nawal mumbled something before she stopped short. Tears spilled from her eyes and ran down her cheeks.

"Oh, I'm sorry! Did I say something wrong?" asked Oona.

Nawal wiped her face with the back of her hand, looking embarrassed.

"It's … it's my family. There's almost no food left either," she stammered bitterly. "But you live in Los Angeles and probably can't understand that," she said, narrowing her eyes, which started to glint with resentment.

Oona remained silent. Now she understood why Nawal was so cold toward her. She assumed that Oona's life was easy and carefree simply because she lived in a developed country, and in California no less.

"Nawal!" scolded Aqiwo, turning toward the two girls. "Remember what Thothan said: 'Don't judge by appearances.' You never know what difficulties others are experiencing!"

Oona trembled and felt a lump in her throat. This was the first time someone had stood up for her. That someone had protected her.

"My parents are farmers and there hasn't been a harvest for over a year! Our entire village is starving to death!" Nawal pursued, her eyes shooting daggers at Oona and Aqiwo.

Oona stopped herself from asking if she knew what it was like not to have a family. To be all alone. She wanted to shout that at least Nawal had come from a gentle and loving home. But, while she was having trouble controlling her emotions, she had to admit that her problems could hardly be compared to the other girl's. She stole a glance at Aqiwo to gauge his reaction. He was looking at her compassionately, his eyes glowing. Oona immediately lowered her head. But she could tell that Nawal had a puzzled look on her face, as if she didn't know what to think. In any case, the glint of resentment that had flashed in her eyes seemed to have disappeared.

"I'm sorry, Oona. The desert is eating our country. My father and brother went into town about two weeks ago to find a solution, a job, anything. But they never returned! We don't know what happened to them, so I'm kind of on edge."

"I'm sorry too," Oona murmured. "Did you notify the police?"

"The police don't come to our village. We're too poor for them to care about us. No one cares about us," she wailed.

"We'll find them. Eterna will help us!" cried Aqiwo.

Nawal smiled faintly, her jade-colored eyes now shining with a glimmer of hope.

A few moments later, the three young Guardians struggled to the top of a gigantic dune. Oona's jaw dropped. Before her rose the three colossal pyramids of Giza, a trio of queens sparkling brightly amid mortals: the formidable guardians of the sacred land and the Nile, extending their noble wings up to the sun as if invoking the heavens. Their summits were like the tips of a royal crown piercing the bright blue sky above the Great Sphinx. Glorious. Sublime. One of the Seven Wonders of the World.

The air shimmered in the heat. A few steps away from them, right in the middle of the dunes, stood a plant, apparently defying the infinity of sand.

"A cactus!" Oona called out.

"I think your thirst is making you delirious," Aqiwo retorted.

Oona covered her parched mouth with the back of her hand and approached the plant.

"If Oona's delirious, then I am too," said Nawal, pointing to the small tree with fierce balls of thorns. "But it can't be a cactus since there are no cactuses in Egypt!"

Instinctively, Oona lifted her hands toward the plant which split down the center, releasing water. Wide-eyed, she shook her head, then cupped her hands below the spiny, paddle-shaped leaves.

"But … how did you do that?" asked Aqiwo, amazed.

"I don't know, but I stopped asking questions a long time ago," she mumbled, quickly bringing the water to her mouth so as not to waste the precious liquid. The effect of the first drops to reach her lips and moisten her throat was like an electric current going through her. Immediately, all the cells of her body seemed to quiver and revive.

Nawal and Aqiwo joined her as the blazing sun started to sink below the horizon. Suddenly, a green valley appeared amid the rays of the setting sun to gradually reveal Eterna, who was covered in moss and flowers, with her lips the color of seafoam and her eyebrows pine green. The goddess was lying beneath an umbrella of shimmering rainbows, wrapping ferns around some the lifeless branches in her hair.

"*Min tolthi*, I see you are becoming familiar with the desert. Know that even if you can't see me, I am always with you," she declared, tilting her gigantic head toward the small tree.

"So, what you're saying is that … it's because of you there's a cactus that is not a cactus in the middle of the desert?" Oona queried.

"As long as I'm alive, Nature will protect you," she affirmed.

At the sound of these comforting words, a strange warmth filled Oona's heart. Despite the thousand and one dangers that awaited her, she felt safe for the first time in a long while. She wished she could hug Eterna.

"Was it you who helped me cut the cactus in half?" asked Oona.

"The elements of nature respond to your wishes, my child."

So, she had the power to control water, air, fire, and earth at will?

"Really?" she couldn't help but say aloud.

The emerald-colored goddess nodded, and a host of tropical Java sparrows escaped from the luxurious vegetation of her hair to twirl in the sky.

"I do not know for how long, alas. I am fading," Eterna added, shivering.

Oona shuddered.

"Then we must hurry!" exclaimed Oona, sensing a shadow looming over her. The white eagle hovered above them, his immense wingspan stretching across several sand dunes.

"Thothan!" Aqiwo cried as the dazzling eagle landing on Eterna's shoulder of ferns.

"Tonight, when the moon reaches its height among the stars, you will go to meet the Sphinx and answer his riddle," Eterna proclaimed while gazing at the orange sky.

"Meet the Sphinx?" Nawal repeated.

"Yes. According to the Prophecy, Oona will solve his riddle so that you can access the pyramids to find the First Key," she responded, lowering her flowery face toward Oona.

"Do you know the solution to the riddle?" Aqiwo inquired.

Eterna shook her head, causing a shower of pine needles to fall on the sand, now glowing red in the sunset.

"But how will I know what the solution is? And what happens if I don't answer correctly?" Oona asked anxiously.

"The Sphinx is the Guardian of the pyramids' mysteries. He is the embodiment of all the gods, and all their knowledge that is safeguarded within the sacred sanctuaries, and that can only be revealed to the initiated. If you fail to solve his riddle, the doors to the pyramids will be sealed and ..."

Eterna paused and contemplated the trio. She sighed. "And the Sphinx will breathe a poisonous wind on you."

Eterna met Oona's gaze.

"You are our only chance," she added, giving her an empathetic look.

Oona was completely overwhelmed by the idea that their lives might depend on her.

"What a relief," she said sarcastically.

Moments later, the Guardians had collapsed from exhaustion and were already sound asleep on the sand. Oona rolled over on her linen blanket, stirred by a strange dream: in a remote rainforest, a wild boar and his mate were sleeping next to each other in a shallow den that dipped into the ground like a saucer. The canopy of leaves covering their nest started to rustle and the little head of an especially unsightly young boar poked through. He was so ugly that it was endearing. The piglet grunted, then went back to sleep as a dark figure loomed menacingly over his family. At dawn, the little animal woke up and blinked in the first light of dawn. His parents had disappeared! He stared at the empty nest in disbelief. Distressed, he howled in despair, looking around him in every direction. Not far off, a man in glossy black armor was handing the piglet's parents over to a group of hunters with rifles at the ready. Asura!

Oona awoke with a start, opening her eyes to the starry Egyptian sky. Her heartbeat pounded in her ears. Her dream had seemed so real! She thought about the little boar and Asura, wondering what it could have meant. Looking up at the Big Dipper, she noticed that half the stars had vanished! Quickly, she found her star, which was shining with a bluish halo. Her chest rose and she let out a sigh of contentment.

Thothan woke up Nawal and Aqiwo. His white feathers were dancing in the wind that blew among the shadows of the dunes like the flame of a candle amid dark curls of smoke.

"It's time," he announced. "Oona, light the torch."

"Light the torch? How?" she asked, still half-asleep.

"You know how."

Oona looked at him incredulously. Alwilan's little head emerged from the feathers on his neck.

"Concentrate on the wick."

As she gazed at the baby bird, she remembered the episode with the school bus. She sat up straight and stared at the torch, her hands reaching for the wooden handle as the eagle had shown her earlier.

"Like this?" she asked in an uncertain voice.

It seemed as if the head of the torch were looking at her, taunting her.

"I can't," she protested. "Nothing's happening!"

"Picture the torch catching fire, like a drawing you make in your mind."

Oona tried harder. She closed her eyes, focused all her energy on the torch, and hung onto Eterna's words. *The power is in you, the power is in you …* Everyone held their breath. A ray of crimson light appeared on her forehead and her hands started to tingle. Next, a spark flashed at the base of the wick and the torch caught fire. Flabbergasted, Oona stared at her palms, then her friends.

"Good. Follow me," Thothan urged, grabbing the crackling torch. "We have no time to lose."

He led the way toward the Sphinx's ominous shadow. The procession descended the dune in silence, with the moon lighting the way. Then, Thothan spread his immense, luminous wings and the Guardians mounted their celestial steed.

CHAPTER XII
The Riddle of the Sphinx

The Guardians clung to the eagle's white feathers as he flew in the direction of the Sphinx. Alwilan remained tucked in Oona's neck, where he had found refuge before takeoff. The stone creature with a lion's body and a human's face, a powerful symbol of ferocity and intelligence, rose mightily before the Great Pyramids. Thothan landed in front of the magnificent ruler's gigantic paws, stirring up swirls of sand. The Guardians leapt to the ground.

"Thothan, it's been centuries," the Sphinx teased.

The eagle bowed before the statue, his eyes fixed on the ground.

"I've been waiting for you," the Sphinx boomed in a low, deep voice that sounded as if it had come from another world, his limestone eyes glinting.

Oona approached cautiously. She didn't know whether to curtsy or kneel before him.

Coming to life, the Sphinx lowered its enormous head, triggering an avalanche of sand that rained down on the young adventurers. Oona turned toward the all-powerful statue.

"Great Sphinx of Giza, we've come to ask you to … umm … to let us enter the pyramids," she said, closing her eyes to keep out the grains of sand swirling around her.

The Guardians dusted off their clothes. The Sphinx blew hot air from his huge mouth, causing them to stagger backwards.

"Solve my riddle, or Anubis will escort you to the gates of the Afterlife," threatened the demigod.

Anubis was standing beside the masterful guardian of the pyramids. He had the head of a jackal, covered with fur as black as a moonless night, and a chiseled human body with bulging muscles flexing beneath his golden skin. The absolute peace emanating from the Egyptian god's onyx eyes contrasted with his fatal power, like the very promise of life after death.

"If you die, your souls will be judged by the weight of your hearts, which will determine your destiny in the spirit realm," he stated in a tone devoid of all mercy.

"If your heart weighs the same as the feather of truth, then you will become immortal. If your heart is impure, it will be devoured by the goddess Ammit."

Oona remembered an image of the deity she'd seen in a book on ancient Egypt that showed her with the forequarters of a lion, the hindquarters of a hippopotamus, and the head of a crocodile. She shuddered.

Holding the golden scales for weighing hearts, Anubis nodded gravely. Oona glanced worriedly at her friends and took a deep breath.

"Great Sphinx, please ask your question," she said, quaking inwardly.

"Some say I am flat, others maintain that I am made of water; but, as time will show, I will be the Mother to all of you for eternity. Try to guess my name."

Oona hesitated. Anubis looked up at the Moon, his black fur shimmering in the silver light.

"Answer before Anubis tears your heart out," the Sphinx warned.

Alwilan let out a little squeak.

"Why isn't she answering?" Nawal whispered anxiously to Aqiwo.

"Wait!" cried Oona.

"Waiting is my fate," laughed the statue.

"Is it Life?" she wondered in a small, uncertain voice, her mind racing.

The Sphinx reared up on his colossal legs and roared with the force of an earthquake. Oona staggered and fell to the ground. " … *It's not life … or the ocean … or humanity …*" she repeated to herself, panting, as different answers whirled around in her mind.

The Sphinx took a deep breath and started to exhale a wind that became more and more violent with every second. Anubis stepped forward. *The poisoned wind!* thought Oona, remembering Eterna's words.

"Wait! I know …" she exclaimed, coughing. "It's … it's the Earth!" she shouted, suddenly sure of the answer.

Abruptly, the ground stopped shaking. The Sphinx went back down on all fours, his body turning once again to stone. Anubis withdrew to a golden alcove behind one of the statue's paws while an immense portal of sand opened out of thin air before the sacred tomb, revealing a mosaic of stars hanging in the cloudless night sky.

"Welcome to the kingdom of the gods and the secrets of all things," said the Sphinx.

Chapter XIII
The First Key

Through the portal of sand, the explorers could see an immense arch covered with endless rows of colorful hieroglyphs, like a rainbow of mysterious tales. The Guardians gazed in awe at the holy writings.

"The Egyptians believe that these are the words of the gods," Nawal murmured in wonderment.

The trio advanced through the sacred archway. In front of the pyramids was a circular building. In the center of the building stood a granite altar on which several tablets and papyrus scrolls were ceremoniously arranged. The altar was positioned immediately below a huge dome covered with hieroglyphs. Oona noticed a torch standing in a sconce next to the majestic pedestal. She approached, held her hands out toward the torch and concentrated with all her strength until a spark flashed, signaling that the wick was ignited. Beaming with pride, she realized she was starting to master her power! Taking the torch, she leaned over to shine its light on the middle scroll, a kind of ancient map. It showed three secret passages hidden behind the altar. Aqiwo traced a route on the map with his index finger.

"This gallery leads …" he began, sliding his finger over the dried leaf, " …to the pyramid of … Alnilam. This one goes to the pyramid of Alnitak, and the third to the pyramid of Mintaka."

The moonlight poured through an opening in the domed roof. Oona looked through the carefully chiseled gap in the rock and could see the constellation of Orion's belt shining above.

"Look! The three pyramids are directly below the three stars of Orion's belt, just like the three dots on our arms," she exclaimed. "But how did you know their names, Aqiwo?"

"My grandmother would teach us the names of the stars every night around the fire," he said nostalgically. "She was the one who raised me, after …" he said, lowering his voice and looking down. "Anyway, Oona, what were you saying about our tattoos?"

Oona sensed that something terrible must have happened to him and longed to give him a comforting hug. Her heart swelled with tenderness. And he was interested in the stars, just like her!

"Each dot must represent a pyramid," she said enthusiastically as she examined the markings on her skin. "And, according to mine, my key should be … inside the pyramid of Alnilam, right below Alnilam, the brightest star in the constellation of Orion!" she concluded, as excited as an explorer making a discovery.

"Mine should be in the pyramid of Alnitak," Nawal said delightedly, peering at her own markings.

"And mine is in Mintaka!" Aqiwo exclaimed as he stared at his forearm. "Maybe we should split up and meet later, after we've each explored our pyramid?"

"I'm not sure that's a good idea, Aqiwo; it could be dangerous, right?"

"Yes, what are we going to do if Asura comes after us?"

Oona felt a flutter of fear in her stomach.

"I agree, but we'll lose too much time if we stay together to explore the pyramids, one after the other. And it would be foolish of Asura to come after us before we find the Three Keys!"

"You're right," Oona agreed as she lit two more torches and handed them to her companions. "But whatever happens, let's be on our guard and meet back here before the sun rises."

"Well, this is where we go our separate ways," she concluded, apprehensively. "Be careful and good luck!" she said. She stretched one of her hands out toward her companions, a mute invitation for them to put their hand on hers as a way of acknowledging their common purpose.

Nawal stared at her and, for the first time, her sea-green eyes lit up with a flash of solidarity. The girl placed a tense hand on Oona's, then relaxed her fingers. Oona smiled at her, glad of this small sign of friendship. Aqiwo gave them a contented look and smiled broadly before covering the girls' hands with his own. Oona trembled. Their destinies were linked, and now Aqiwo was a part of her life. She felt her cheeks getting hot and secretly prayed he wouldn't notice anything.

Then she grabbed the papyrus, and the Guardians separated. Oona hurried down a dark passage inside the pyramid of Alnilam, her torch dimly lighting her way. Suddenly, she thought she could see shadows dancing on the tunnel's damp walls, and then her torch went out … Her blood ran cold! She had the distinct feeling that she was being followed by something or someone. Her claustrophobia kicked in as her insides twisted in terror. Damned torch! Oona resisted the fear with all her might, visualizing the passage being inundated with light. A small flame flickered and then the wick finally rekindled. She turned around, her heart pounding inside her chest. In the dim light, she was only able to make out a series of pictograms painted in faded colors along the walls. Her anxiety must have been playing tricks on her because she couldn't see anyone! After getting lost several times in the subterranean labyrinth, she finally entered an enormous chamber that glimmered in the flickering torch light with a thousand shades of bronze. It was shaped like a pyramid and supported by a massive ice pillar. As she gazed at it in wonder, she felt a warm point of light forming on her forehead. *Oona, Oonaaa …* It was Aqiwo's voice! She couldn't see him, but she could hear him as if he were standing right next to her.

"Aqiwo?!" she called out in surprise, her voice echoing eerily inside the vast chamber.

"Yes, it's me!"

"Are you okay? I can hear you!" she laughed.

"I can hear you, too! I can hear both of you!" shouted Nawal.

"Everything is fine, I just think I'm seeing mummies everywhere," he joked uneasily.

"Wow, our minds are 'talking' to each other!" marveled Oona, who had always been fascinated by telepathy.

Peering ahead, she saw sacred engravings representing the phases of the moon carved into a granite doorway. She placed her hand on them.

Suddenly, her right foot went through a hole in the floor, which had been covered by cobwebs and a pile of dust. She lost her balance, then cried out as she caught hold of the door handle, just in time to stop herself from falling through the hole.

"Oona! Is everything okay?" shouted Aqiwo.

"Yes, it's a trap," she panted. "Be careful, they're probably all over," she warned them, bending down to pick up a stone.

Oona threw the stone into the newly revealed opening but heard nothing in response. She examined the abyss cautiously and thought she heard strange noises coming from the dark hole. She threw light on the ominous excavation and was horrified to discover that the floor was covered with scorpions, their silhouettes visible in the dark and their venomous stingers poised to attack,.

"In Alnilam, the ground is covered with scorpions!" she warned them, the dot on her forehead heating up.

"Yes, there are scorpions everywhere here, too!" Aqiwo shrieked.

As he spoke, legions of scorpions swarmed the royal tomb. Oona compared her golden tattoo with the design on the walls of Alnilam's chamber, which depicted a triangle within a circle. *Another triangle? Could it be another pyramid?* Questions raced through Oona's mind as she tried not to panic at the sight of the arachnids advancing toward her, their long, curved tails striking the air in search of prey.

"This is it! I'm in the mastaba!" Nawal shouted.

"The what?" asked Aqiwo.

"The mastaba, the tomb! Oona, where's the key?" she asked, her voice trembling. She was probably having to deal with unexpected enemies, too.

Oona continued to back away from the scorpions, which were advancing steadily in her direction. A ray of light fell on her as she stepped on an equilateral triangle etched into the ground. As soon as her feet found the center of the figure, rays of blinding light shot up from each of the triangle's three sides to form a pyramid of light around her. A geyser of otherworldly symbols gushed down from the top of the glittering column toward her head. She shuddered with pleasure as the light from the pyramid seemed to infuse each of her cells with well-being. The ground trembled and the ice pillar started to melt, causing the arachnids to retreat. Mystified, Oona widened her eyes, her mouth agape. Suddenly she clapped her hands, then looked at the papyrus map.

"I've got it!" she shouted, studying the map. "Go until you find the sarcophagus chamber with a pillar of ice! According to the map, there should be one in each pyramid. Find the triangle in the farthest corner and stand in the middle without moving!"

Oona heard nothing in return.

"Nawal? Aqiwo? Are you there? Is everything OK?

There was nothing but deathly silence.

Suddenly: "There are scorpions everywhere!" Nawal shouted, panicked. "Ah, the triangle!"

"Aqiwo, is everything okay?" Oona persisted. "Our body is the First Key!"

"What do you mean?" Aqiwo yelled breathlessly.

"Our bodies are the keys of the pyramids," she replied eagerly. "You just have to get inside the triangle!"

The walls of the three adjacent chambers collapsed around her to reveal Nawal and Aqiwo, who had passed through underground tunnels to end up standing beside each other. Their eyes were closed. Aqiwo was in the center of the Mintaka triangle with a pyramid of light flickering around him and his face beaming with enchantment. Nawal was also standing inside a glowing pyramid.

Exposed now to the blistering Sahara sun, the remaining pillars of ice melted instantly, and the poisonous arachnids were submerged in a shower of icy water. Aqiwo pointed his finger at the outline of a door drenched in sunlight. In the doorway appeared the silhouette of a man with a falcon's head adorned with the golden disk of the Sun and a rearing cobra.

"Look! He looks like … Ra, the Egyptian god!" whispered the young boy.

"Where?" asked Oona.

The Sun blinded them, and the vision of the god vanished, like an apparition from another world.

"He was right there! Unless I was hallucinating!" Aqiwo said, astounded.

Rays from the sun entered through evenly spaced light shafts above and were projected onto the tiled floor: the mosaic of tiles seemed to form a complex pattern that looked like a mysterious symbol. The symbol rose into the air and flickered near Oona's forearm as the Guardians' triangular shafts of light disintegrated.

"Look! The markings on my arm have changed!" said Oona in astonishment, pointing to the golden inscriptions. "Now it looks like a series of numbers."

Nawal leaned toward her.

"Those are geographic coordinates," she declared. "Yes, that's what they are. Now that we've determined that we're the First Key, Eterna's clues will tell us what the next step is. Just a second … 34.341568 is the latitude, and 108.940178 the longitude for …" Nawal paused, thinking intently. "Xi'An, China!"

Oona saw that her tattoo was starting to blur and that the ink of the three golden dots on her skin was fading. Now that the trio has solved the riddle of the

First Key, the dots representing the pyramids were disappearing. The Guardians looked at their arms: just a triangle and the mysterious symbol were still visible next to the coordinates.

A dark veil rose from behind the dancing hologram and obscured the sun. Astera's cruel eyes opened wide, and the Egyptian plains resonated with a hollow sound: "China! So that's where the Supreme Crystal is. Thank you, stupid Guardians!" sneered the spirit of the Dark Planet. "And now, perish! All of you!" she shouted as myriads of scorpions rained down from her veil.

"Oh, no! Not again! What a nightmare!" protested Nawal, shuddering with terror at the sight of the arachnids that were descending like hail just a few meters away.

Oona took the papyrus out of her pocket and took a quick glance at the map. "This way!" she shouted, rushing toward a dark passage.

Nawal and Aqiwo followed her, and they ran to a golden staircase that led to the Sphinx's head. Aqiwo and Oona emerged in the Sphinx's left eye while Nawal appeared in the other one. More than a hundred feet above the ground, the Guardians' breath was taken away by the sight of the desert floor covered in scorpions, moving relentlessly forward, about to climb the ancient statue's gigantic front paws.

"When enemies are too strong, trick them," Aqiwo recited in a meditative voice.

Oona and Nawal looked at him quizzically as the deadly insects scuttled ever closer.

"It's a Chumash thing," he said evasively, smiling. "When enemies are too strong, you must deceive them. Using force won't work."

Grimacing with disgust, Nawal kicked away the first scorpions that had just reached her refuge.

"Does anyone have another brilliant idea? We need it fast!" she moaned, horrified.

With her hands clasped on her chest in prayer, Oona stared into the distance. She had been feeling a new kind of strength since her Key had been activated, as if carried toward her on a wave from the universe. She took a deep breath and stretched her arms toward the sun. *The Power is in you, the Power is in you …*

"O Wind, I summon you now! We are the children of Eterna, the Guardians of Earth! We need your help!"

Instantly, in answer to her summons, a powerful wind rose up and blew across the desert. The gusts suddenly intensified, and clouds of dust rolled across the copper sky, dropping a deluge of sand on the dreadful army. Visibility was practically zero.

"Deploy your venom!" a livid Astera ordered the scorpions from the sky.

The storm was so violent that the Sphinx was now almost completely covered in sand, and a new dune was forming at his feet. The trio escaped from his eyes by leaping out and then surfing down the hill of sand. Oona fell behind and found herself right in the middle of the legions of scorpions.

"Oona!" shouted Aqiwo, turning around.

"The whales …!" she shouted in horror.

Suddenly, she fell to her knees and let out a heart-rending cry.

"Give me your hand!" Aqiwo yelled, braving the blizzard of sand to approach her.

Nawal turned around and, to her horror, realized that hundreds of scorpions were only a few inches away from Oona, with their stingers aimed directly at her. Aqiwo tried desperately to grab Oona's hand as she stretched her fingers toward him, but the strong wind blew him back and their fingers couldn't connect.

"The whales …! They're telling me that they're under attack in the port of Guoyuan in Chongqing, China," Oona screamed, horrified.

She closed her eyes and concentrated as hard as she could, calling on the forces of the desert for help. Her invocation was like a prayer: "Fauna and flora of the desert, water, air and fire, I implore you, I need your help!" Channeling the whales as she had before, she let out a long, shrill wail. In response to her primitive cry, she heard a rumbling roar and, suddenly, a camel appeared out of the blizzard. Galloping up to her, the ungulate knelt down next to her and, with a nudge of its muzzle, invited her to climb up on its back. Oona struggled to her feet, braving the gusts of sand, and climbed onto its hump. The animal then rose quickly to its feet and carried her over the scorpions. She squinted and gave a faint smile. "Thank you!" she communicated telepathically to the animal, before letting out another devastating wail.

"Oona, what are the whales saying?" Nawal shouted, shielding her eyes with the back of her hand.

"Astera has just arrived in China!" Oona shouted. She clung to the camel as it came to a stop alongside her companions.

"Give me your hand!" Aqiwo said to his two friends.

With the sand pelting their faces, the Guardians reached out for each other, extending their arms as far as they could. Oona's cheeks were burning from the storm and her lashes were getting so encrusted with sand that she could scarcely open her eyes. Her hand was whipped by the sand as she reached out blindly. At last, the tips of their fingers touched.

CHAPTER XIV
The Forest of Spirits

Three translucent bubbles rose up amid the turbulent winds, leaving the sandstorm and the Dark Planet's poisonous army behind. Gliding through the air at top speed, the Guardians flew over the Red Sea, the mountains of Yemen, the Indian Ocean, the glittering skyscrapers of Mumbai and West Bengal, and the foothills of the Himalayas until, finally, they saw Beijing, the capital of China. Oona's eyes grew wide as she contemplated the sight unfolding beneath her feet, remembering how often she had dreamed of discovering the world beyond her books! They passed over the Forbidden City and the majestic saffron-colored roofs flashed under her until they reached the Gate of Heavenly Peace, the Temple of Tranquility, and Tiananmen Square, all partially obscured by a thick cloud of pollution. Then, the trio glided over the Great Wall of China, one of the ancient wonders of the world, originally extending more than thirteen thousand miles across the country.

"The Dragon of the Earth ..." Oona whispered.

The gigantic wall wound its way through the lush valleys of the Middle Kingdom like a fantastical stone serpent. At dusk, the bubbles began to descend, meaning the Guardians would have to find a clearing and prepare to land. The wall was, as Oona had read in one of her books on Asia, situated along the border of the Spirit Forest in Henan Province, about sixty-two miles from Luoyang and the White Horse Temple. Located in the center of China, Luoyang was one of the four ancient capitals of the Middle Kingdom and considered the cradle of Chinese civilization. The spheres were now rolling over a sea of bamboo whose leaves danced hypnotically beneath them.

Shortly after they bubbles had dropped them in a clearing and burst, Aqiwo was already using dead leaves to prepare some makeshift beds, while Oona and Nawal picked a kind of large black fruit from a nearby tree.

"The color isn't very appetizing," Oona exclaimed, rotating one of the fruits between her fingers. "Nawal, are you sure we can eat them?"

"Yes, they're black persimmons. You'll see, they're delicious," she replied, laughing. "Oona, can I ask you something?"

"Yes?"

"Were you the one who summoned the camel to come to your rescue?"

Embarrassed, Oona winced inwardly.

"That's so amazing!"

Oona smiled to herself, feeling that a bond of friendship was blossoming between them, enabling them to move past their previous prejudices.

Suddenly, a little ball of black and white fur burst out from the bushes: a baby panda, gorging itself on fruit! Black persimmon juice was smeared around its mouth and dripping down its snow-white fur.

"Aw, it's so cute!" exclaimed Oona.

The little bear stuffed another persimmon into its mouth, letting out little cries of delight.

"See? Even pandas love persimmons!" Nawal exclaimed, clapping her hands.

"Are you lost? Where are your parents?" Oona asked the little animal.

The adorable creature, which bore a strong resemblance to a stuffie, opened its eyes wide and squeaked. Oona felt a wave of concern rush over her.

"It must have lost its way in the bamboo maze," Aqiwo said.

Oona petted the panda affectionately. Its coat was so soft. She looked into its eyes to reassure it, and a burst of unconditional love made her heart leap in her chest.

"In Chumash culture, bears are the guardians of men," Aqiwo said. "We should sleep side by side. The night's going to be cool," he added, patting the baby bear on the head.

Before long, Aqiwo and Nawal had fallen asleep, but Oona lay awake, with the bear cub snuggled against her chest, gazing up at the starry sky in awe and fear. Suddenly, her star started to flash, as if to remind her that she wasn't alone, and this eased her mind.

How her universe had changed in just two days! It was as if her life on Earth was already a thing of the past: time seemed to have sped up in a way that was as amazing as it was irreversible. With a pang of guilt, she realized that she had temporarily forgotten all about her mother. Oddly enough, despite the dangers, Oona felt that she had found her place, and she felt filled with a sense of peace despite the prevailing chaos. It remained to be seen if she would be up to the job of saving Eterna. The panda sighed in its sleep and added to her feeling of calm. Comforted by its warmth and steady heartbeat, she drifted off to sleep.

The quiet of the night was suddenly shattered by a high-pitched wail. Aqiwo sat bolt upright in his bed. The baby panda whimpered in panic.

"Shh," Oona breathed softly.

"What's happening?" fretted Nawal, bleary-eyed with sleep.

Oona saw silver foxes, rabbits, white wolves, and snow leopards darting past them without even noticing their presence. As they fled in panic, their terror made her blood run cold.

"Animals know when danger is coming. I think we should follow them," Aqiwo said while his eyes started to close …

What's the matter with him? Oona wondered, taken aback. *This isn't the time to fall asleep!* Tremors coursed through the body of the young Chumash and beads of sweat rolled down his forehead.

"Aqiwo?!" Oona cried out, alarmed.

He stood up.

"It's Asura …! I saw … I saw the eyes of the Dark Planet … then an explosion of flames," he stammered, panicked, looking as if he wanted to drive away these disturbing visions with a wave of his hand. He seemed to be in a state of shock. "I also heard Eterna's voice," he continued. "She told me that I've been given the power to see the truth and read people's life story in their eyes."

Above them, langurs, golden snub-nosed monkeys, macaques, and a colony of birds were all fleeing in the same direction, as if life itself were abandoning the forest in the face of imminent danger.

"We should go!" he announced forcefully.

The Guardians were surrounded by flitting shadows and fearful cries. Oona tried desperately to grab hold of the panicked baby panda, which was jumping around in all directions.

"We've got to go now, Oona!" insisted Aqiwo.

She finally managed to wrestle the little ball of black and white fur to the ground.

"I'm coming!" she shouted, picking up the little bear in her arms.

Nawal was leading the trio and followed the wild animals toward an unknown destination. Oona was running behind Aqiwo with the bear clinging to her neck. Their frantic flight through the forest led them to the edge of a dizzyingly high cliff. In the gorge below, a blue-green waterfall was pounding against the rocks. Nawal jumped off the cliff's edge and flew over the thundering torrent without a moment's hesitation. Aqiwo made his way purposefully toward the precipice. How could they not be afraid of the void? *So much for being a Guardian of the Earth!* As the Guardian of the Waters, Nawal was already swimming like a wild salmon in the turbulent river. Oona suddenly felt overcome by doubts and discouragement. What if she couldn't do it? What if she was unable to accomplish her mission? She hated herself for being so weak! Just then, something stopped her in her tracks: a gigantic panda was blocking her way, standing on its hind legs with arms outstretched.

The animal began to roar ferociously. Oona's blood went cold and her heart trembled. She could feel the Chinese bear's despair – that of a mother whose child has been taken away – tearing at her insides. She froze in fear, but then … a realization!

"Oh, look who's here," Oona murmured in the cub's ear as she gently placed it on the ground, all the while, keeping her eyes fixed on its mother, who seemed ready to strike her down.

The mother bear seemed reassured as she stared into Oona's eyes. She grabbed her little one with a paw, grunting with pleasure. Oona felt her muscles relax and was able to breathe again. All the same, she remained motionless to avoid any misunderstandings. The cub lavishly licked its mother's muzzle, then freed itself from her embrace to frolic playfully at her feet, squealing like a little monkey. Their reunion made Oona smile with happiness, despite the close call she'd just had.

"*Oona! Oonaaaa!*" Aqiwo yelled out, sounding panicked. Oona backed away from the bears, then came out from behind a shrub to join Aqiwo, who was standing at the cliff's edge.

"I thought we'd lost you!" he blustered, though also looking relieved.

"I'm sorry," she replied apologetically. "I had to get the baby panda back to its mother."

The powerful current of water bordered with foam fell freely for several hundred feet before crashing into the yellow river below. Nawal was waiting for them in the water, hanging onto a trunk that was stuck near the river's edge. The Guardian of the Waters seemed to speak to the rapids. Maybe she was instructing them to be gentle with her friends.

Paralyzed, Oona gazed at the vertical drop. Aqiwo held his hand out to her. She sighed and stretched her fingers toward his. The contact between their hands made a bluish spark, followed by a wave of multicolored particles that rose in glittering spirals toward the sky. Oona noticed that there were places where the skin on her arm was glowing. What was going on? She didn't have the time to give it any further thought because she found herself toe to toe with Aqiwo, who was so close that their faces almost touched. He was looking at her with his glowing eyes, setting her heart on fire. Oona felt a new emotion wash over her and her cheeks grew hot. Words were unnecessary; they didn't need to speak.

"I'm sorry," he said in a tone of deep compassion, his eyes expressing great sadness.

Of course! She had forgotten that he had the power to read a person's entire life story in their eyes! She looked away immediately. Had he been able to read the emotion she felt toward him? Embarrassment was quickly replaced by shame. Had he been able to see her mother's erratic behavior? Her father's explosions? No, she mustn't let him see all that. Anything but that! She didn't dare raise her eyes, for fear of rejection.

"What did you see?" she asked, dejectedly.

"Why are you ashamed?

"I guess … It's just that … I don't have a very normal family," she replied in a whisper, her face expressionless.

"Who *does* have a normal family?" he asked, rhetorically. "You aren't your family, you know, and you can choose a new one if you wish!" he added, his tone softening.

A faint smile played on Oona's lips. But what exactly had he seen? Had he seen her mother barge into class one day, claiming that spies on her father's payroll might kidnap Oona? Had he seen her plastering artificial snow on the neighbors' windows, because she didn't see any reason not to celebrate Christmas every day? Worse, had he seen her father call her names she preferred to bury in the depths of her memory? And the nights when she was locked in her room and it seemed like she would never stop crying – had he seen that? Fearing rejection, she'd spent her childhood pretending that everything was fine. And he was right: she hadn't chosen her parents. But despite that, she could still feel the sting of betrayal in her chest. But, it seemed like perhaps Aqiwo accepted her for who she really was. At that realization, some of the burden that had weighed her down for so long was lifted, as if by magic, and sobs rose in her throat. Just then, a golden pheasant flew past them, bringing her back to reality.

"And you, Aqiwo, why were you raised by your grandmother?" Oona asked, moved.

Aqiwo squinted, then inhaled deeply, as if to give himself courage.

"My parents died in a car accident when I was three years old, so I was raised by my grandmother. I hardly remember them, but she told me that they returned to the Earth, to the sacred trees in our forest."

"Oh, I'm so sorry!" she exclaimed, giving him a hug, and then pulling away. "Oh no … I didn't mean to … I mean," she stammered.

"You can hug me whenever you like!" Aqiwo answered, grinning from ear to ear.

Oona felt like a sun in her body had just started to shine.

"It's time to go, Oona. Do you feel ready to jump?"

Oona leaned over the precipice and her blood chilled at the sight of the drop. She shook her head in resignation.

"Don't worry, I'm here by your side," he continued, his voice comforting her.

There was no way she was going to chicken out in front of him! This new feeling she was experiencing in his presence literally gave her wings. The dawn was sending iridescent rays of light into the waters of the Pearl River. But, at the top of the waterfall, strange plumes of smoke and fleeting shadows crisscrossed the sky. Oona held her breath and closed her eyes, preparing herself for the worst.

The sun was still waking up as the two friends joined hands and jumped into the river. Oona felt the wind blowing through her hair and on her face. It didn't feel to her like she was falling at all, but rather that she was floating on a mattress of cool air. Her body became weightless until the sudden contact with the cold water of the river brought her back to reality. She entered the water so powerfully that she couldn't help frolicking a bit before surfacing in an eddy of bubbles. As her head emerged from the swiftly flowing water at the base of the waterfall, Oona heard a long, harrowing groan – the unbearable cry of a wild animal in distress. Shivering, she looked around, disoriented. She spotted Aqiwo trying unsuccessfully to swim against the current toward her. Then Asura emerged from the dancing shadows of the forest at the top of the waterfall, flanked by the dark silhouette of an animal on four stocky legs. It seemed to be sizing her up. Scared, Oona swallowed some water before being swept away by a current through a narrow channel, closing off the way back to Nawal and Aqiwo. The river appeared to be alive. In spite of how rough the water was, she closed her eyes and focused, trying to become one with the liquid. "Easy, easy," Oona whispered to the stream. "Please help me get back to dry land!" Immediately, the current subsided, giving way to absolute calm.

The trio swam to shore and lay on the sun-warmed rocks, exhausted. Oona was struggling to catch her breath, shivering with cold, and periodically spitting out water. Before them lay the Forest of Spirits, covered with a layer of snow. A light breeze dusted the Guardians with tiny snow crystals that, shaped like six-pointed stars, seemed miraculously designed. Cupping her hands to catch them, Nawal contemplated the fleeting geometric crystals, open-mouthed.

"I've never seen snow before," she marveled, teeth chattering.

On their left, a vast frozen lake fringed with conifers extended its white cloak before a range of terraced mountains range as if it were their magic mirror.

"Shh … we're not alone," whispered Oona, who didn't know if she was trembling from cold or fear, nodding toward the woods.

The Guardians froze as they saw shadows moving in the forest behind them. Aqiwo surveyed their surroundings. The lake was their only option. The boy stepped forward and placed his foot on the frozen surface to test the strength of the ice, eager to go even further. He frowned. Oona glimpsed a branch being pushed aside by one of the dancing shadows, which was soon joined by several others. It was Asura, monstrously tall, a hideous smile etched on his face. Horrified, her entire body was shaking.

"Asura is here!" Oona shouted.

He was walking toward the Guardians, followed by a group of dull-eyed humans who seemed to obey him blindly. The Dark Planet's lava eyes appeared in the sky, as if to observe the fateful meeting. Oona shuddered. A dozen of Asura's slaves were advancing toward the Guardians, knives at the ready. They were surrounded! She tried to control the panic that she could feel rising within her and clouding her thoughts. Just like Master Wada had taught her, she breathed as evenly as possible so as to remain calm. Remembering her lessons, she adopted the kung fu heron stance, with one leg raised and the foot protecting the other knee, ready to kick out at anyone who came near. Nawal and Aqiwo stepped back and assumed the rider's stance, as if they were sitting astride a horse. But it was obvious that they were trapped.

Just then, a man in a yellow cape appeared out of nowhere, landing gracefully between the trio and their attackers. Who was he? Was this stranger a friend or foe? The newcomer stood motionless with his face hidden by a *douli*, the famous Chinese bamboo hat. Asura's soldiers attacked him boldly, but he deftly dodged their assaults, fending them off with a series of lightning-fast jabs from his bamboo stick. Oona couldn't believe her eyes! The man was leaping from one rock to another like a ballet dancer, his saffron-colored kimono whirling in the air. Asura spread his arms and, from his palms, sent out a blinding crimson light. Defying all the laws of gravity, the mysterious figure leapt forward and pushed Asura backwards. Unfortunately, the scarlet wave that missed him struck Aqiwo, who promptly collapsed.

"Aqiwo!" Oona shouted, rushing toward him.

She knelt beside the young boy who was lying on the ground, unconscious. Almost fainting with fear, she could feel anger and despair rising inside her and setting her spirit on fire. She stood up, then, and turned her head toward Asura. She saw his eyes burning with hatred. Eterna's voice filled her mind. *"Transform your anger into strength!"* Oona let out a long, savage scream.

"AHHHHHH!!!!"

A eucalyptus tree near her caught fire. Intuitively, she spread her arms and held both hands out toward Asura. A multicolored wave of energy burst from her palms and whirled in the air before falling on the horde of soldiers. They fell to the ground like a row of dominoes. But her impromptu attack still missed Asura. Oona looked at her hands, stunned. Aqiwo lifted his head.

"Remind me never to make you angry," he murmured in a weak voice.

"Aqiwo! Are you alright?" Oona asked apprehensively as she bent over him, the blood pulsing in her temples.

Aqiwo nodded his head.

"You scared me half to death!" she exclaimed as she placed a hand on his chest, as if to calm the beating of his heart.

Aqiwo had suddenly filled her universe. If she lost him, it felt like she would fall into a black hole.

Asura's slaves were already getting back on their feet, ready to attack again.

Quickly, Nawal launched a bamboo stick with a sharpened tip toward Asura. He narrowly dodged the blade by catching the spear in his right hand, and the Guardians took advantage of his momentary distraction to flee toward the opposite shore. Oona could read the rage on his face. He grabbed his sword but, instead of striking the mysterious stranger who was within reach, chose instead to stab the heavy blade deep into the layer of ice covering the lake. A dark wound formed on the surface and spread out into a multitude of cracks like a spider's web. A black line rushed toward Oona, cracking the ice as it went. Wide-eyed with fear, she turned and ran in the opposite direction from the pursuing rift but skidded and slipped. Unable to grab hold of anything, she screamed in a panic. Too late! The ice opened beneath her feet with a deafening roar.

"Oona! Noooo!!!" Nawal and Aqiwo shouted in unison, already safe ashore.

The gap in the ice swallowed Oona, and the icy water froze her skin and chilled her bones. The cold was so intense that it hurt, with an unbearable pain that crushed her forehead and sent stabbing pains through her legs. Breathless and panicked, a leaden fatigue descended on her after several futile attempts to climb out of the opening. She went under, her movements and her thoughts paralyzed by the cold.

Suddenly, she thought she felt someone touching her neck, and then she was overcome with drowsiness. It was over and she was going to die, she knew it. She thought of Aqiwo's forest; she wondered if she would become a tree, too. Then her vision blurred, and everything went black.

CHAPTER XV
The Prophecy of the Monastery

The next thing she knew, she was woken by her body's violent shivering. Where was she? She couldn't tell because she could hardly even open her eyes. All at once, she remembered rushing to the lake and falling into its icy waters. So, had she survived? Or was this the afterlife?

"We've got to take her to the monastery as quickly as possible," said the man with the Chinese hat.

In spite of the difficult situation, Oona felt like smiling as she recognized Master Wada's voice. But her numb lips prevented her from speaking. With difficulty, she raised her hand and noticed that her skin had turned a purplish-blue. How much time had she spent underwater?

"Don't move!"

It was Asura's voice.

An arrow almost hit a macaque that was swinging on a redwood branch above her. Oona managed to turn her head and saw Asura behind Master Wada who was standing beside Nawal and Aqiwo. The villain was aiming another arrow directly at them. She wanted to scream but the muscles of her mouth were still paralyzed from the cold. It was then that a tremor shook the ground. A gigantic panda galloped across the ice and leapt over the Guardians, blocking Asura's missile. It was the baby panda's mother! The enormous bear went up on her hind legs and bellowed at Asura, towering above him menacingly. She brushed away Asura's bow and arrows with the back of her paw, toppling him to the ground. Furiously, he got back on his feet, and the two opponents locked forces in a merciless battle. The Guardians had to take advantage of this opportunity to escape!

"That way!" Master Wada shouted, waving his hand toward a redwood grove.

The nun picked up Oona in her arms like a disjointed puppet and entered the forest, with Nawal and Aqiwo close behind her. Oona, with her head resting on the Master's bony shoulder, saw Asura crawl on the ground and vanish in a whirl of smoke. Although she could hardly keep her eyes open, she was still worried about what would happen to the panda. Right at that moment, the bear appeared behind a clump of hibiscus. She gave Oona a knowing look, as if she were smiling at her. A wave of warmth flowed through Oona's shivering body and she was overcome by an ineffable sense of peace.

As they passed through a curtain of bright green vegetation, a forest of pagodas appeared at the top of a mountain overlooking the Dengfeng Valley. Oona had read somewhere that this valley was known as the Emerald City of China, the center of heaven and earth. Distant sounds of bells and chimes were carried toward them on the wind. She sensed somehow that this scene, which looked hazy after her close brush with death, had a kind of sanctity. Where was Master Wada taking them?

With her head slumped in the saffron folds of Master Wada's robe, Oona made a superhuman effort to keep her eyes open. She saw a Shaolin Temple that reached up above the clouds behind a high red wall decorated with golden fish. A glorious statue of the Buddha was standing in front of a tower. Then, in the distance she saw dozens of men with shaved heads and wearing long yellow robes who were sitting in the lotus position and chanting in devotion. At the monastery door, a young monk greeted Master Wada and the Guardians deferentially and took Oona in his arms as if she were a doll.

"Follow me," the young monk said affably.

He led the group to the entrance of the Temple's golden pagoda. Inside the dazzling structure, the man laid Oona on an embroidered silk blanket at Master Wada's feet. The tiny old woman placed her hands on the girl's frail body.

"How old are you?" Master Wada asked her patient.

Trembling, Oona glanced at the nun whose eyes were ringed with ancient wrinkles. The terrestrial sphere was rotating in her bluish irises. Oona tried to formulate an answer but was too weak. Succumbing to dizziness, she closed her eyes. When she was able to open them partway again, she saw Nawal and Aqiwo exchanging a look of panic.

"She just turned eleven," Aqiwo said.

Master Wada laughed.

"What's so funny?" Nawal asked, perplexed.

Aqiwo remained silent but elbowed Nawal, looking annoyed. Oona remembered that his grandmother had taught him to show the utmost respect to the elderly and not to question their judgment.

"The friend your heart cherishes is at least five thousand years old," Master Wada said, smiling enigmatically and darting Aqiwo a mischievous look.

Oona could hear every word they were saying and wanted to correct Master Wada, but the fever paralyzed her body and the best she could do was let out a little moan. The sage locked her hands on her solar plexus and, in spite of her fever, Oona could feel her cheeks warming.

"Her chi is very weak," Master Wada announced.

"Her what?" asked Aqiwo.

"Her life force."

The Venerable Elder made a few fluid movements in the air over Oona's head and chest. She felt a warm, velvety softness move throughout her body, which calmed her trembling and lightened her heart. Then the Master got up and burned a stick of incense in front of the Buddha. A halo of diffuse light surrounded her, so she resembled a giant firefly glowing in the dark. The young monk prostrated himself and touched his forehead to the ground before the sacred effigy.

"I've transmitted light to her, but I'm afraid it's not enough," Master Wada said in a voice that betrayed her concern.

Suddenly, Oona could barely breathe and curled up into a ball.

"What do you mean? What can we do?" Aqiwo asked, panicking.

The old woman stared hard at her guests, then transferred her gaze to the young monk, whom she looked at with deliberate insistence. He bowed and disappeared behind a lacquered wooden door. When he returned, he was carrying a cushion decorated with pink flamingos and topped with a glittering black pearl. The Venerable Elder placed the pearl on Oona's heart.

"The pearl can save her, but only if her spirit conquers her sadness."

Oona struggled to raise her head. Within the pearl, lightning bolts tore through dancing shadows and fought against the darkness. So, this shadowy, moving mass represented all her sadness? Bitterly, she contemplated the shape of her sorrow as it had materialized in the pearl. This was the invisible, overwhelming force that had weighed her down so many times, swallowing her light and crushing her chest. It seemed to her that all her unhappy memories were concentrated in this dark magma that kept her trapped in misery.

"She's too sad," Master Wada intoned. "She must let it go in order to feel hope. She must believe that she can be worthy of love," she continued, looking at Nawal and Aqiwo as she took Oona's hand.

"Oona, don't be sad!" said Aqiwo, bringing his face close to hers.

His eyes were wide open, like two golden lagoons that seemed to invite her to dive in and leave her miserable past behind. Aqiwo's gaze expressed infinite affection and concern.

"You're not alone, Oona. Remember Cosmos! He loves you so much that he learned how to fly!" Aqiwo implored.

But, she thought immediately, Cosmos was Thothan's son. He had a father and didn't need anyone. But she was no one's daughter!.

"Yes, Oona, even camels are your friends!" added Nawal, dabbing Oona's forehead with a wet towel. "And I'm so sorry, I was wrong about you," she sobbed. "Now we're friends!"

But it was as if Oona were behind an invisible wall that her companions' words couldn't penetrate. She was five years old again, on the ski slope being lashed by the blizzard as her father abandoned her. Despite her cries, his back gradually grew smaller and smaller until it became a black dot in the distance and then disappeared into the whiteness of the mountain. He hadn't even turned around. He wasn't waiting for her. Worse, she remembered his sardonic laughter as the firefighters brought her home. "Children are such a pain!" he'd griped. Devastated, Oona was falling into a black pit. Her eyes half-closed, she saw the shadows filling the bright cracks inside the pearl.

"No, no, no …" Aqiwo stammered. "Remember, Oona, you are not your family!" he implored, taking her hand.

The warm, soft touch of his palm made her tremble, and slowed her descent into the abyss.

"Remember what we said to each other at the top of the cliff this morning," the young boy continued passionately. "Don't be sad! I see you! I know who you are, and I love you just as you are!"

At these words, Oona's eyes opened wide. Aqiwo was looking at her through a mist of tears. A glimmer of light shone in her oblivion only to be eclipsed immediately by a dark swirl. An anvil was crushing Oona's brain, as it reluctantly relived a thousand increasingly sad scenes. Why was her father so cruel? What had she done wrong? Was it because he had a pacemaker instead of a heart? His plastic heart emitted a steady tick-tick all day long, like a time bomb. The man without a heart. And when would she find out where her mother was? With her mother gone, now Oona was truly alone in the world. Without a family. Lost.

"Oona, I don't have any parents, either. If you want, I can be your family?" Aqiwo persisted, pressing his fingers against her hand. "Can you hear me? Oona, please! Answer me!"

"Yes, I can be your family too, Oona!" Nawal chimed in.

The boy let his head fall on Oona's chest. He was crying. Aqiwo and Nawal's words danced like birds of light in Oona's pit of sadness. A burst of hope made her open her eyes, and a flash of light shimmered briefly in the pearl, but then it grew dark again.

"Oona, the shadows in the pearl are growing. You'll die if your mind doesn't fight!" the young boy protested. "Think of everything you've been through! Your spirit is strong, I know it!"

But Oona's thoughts started to wander. She thought back to the bodies of the fish that, as victims of man-made pollution, had washed up on the banks of the Blue River, and then to the panicked polar bear in Eterna's sphere, clinging to the shrinking ice. Sadness engulfed her.

"Eterna needs you, and we're your new family!" Aqiwo insisted. "Please, you can't leave me alone!"

Suddenly, Eterna's loving face filled the screen of Oona's thoughts. The goddess was looking at her tenderly. Oona felt a marvelous power emanating from her presence, a nameless gentleness that gradually filled her with serenity and happiness. Her well of tears was illuminated by a shining light. Oona gathered all the courage she could find in her heart and focused on the image of her new celestial mother and the luminous birds surrounding her, driving away the storm clouds of her gloomy thoughts. A radiant sun started to shine in the blue sky of her mind, filling her suddenly light heart with joy. She even stifled a laugh! Her sadness was a mirage, an illusion of the mind! All she had to do was control her thoughts, she thought, choose them like when she picked berries in the woods. Serene, Oona let herself be rocked by Eterna's warm and velvety embrace. Then she blinked open her eyes.

"The ancient Prophecy …" the old woman murmured, bowing before the precious pearl as if hypnotized.

Like twin black and white waves, the yin and yang symbols appeared from the depths of the lustrous sphere. Master Wada's eyes widened. The two-toned ripples danced inside the pearl until the two patterns joined as one. Oona was saved!

"Aqiwo …?" Oona gasped.

He rushed to her and took her in his arms.

"Oona, are you okay? How are you feeling?" asked Nawal.

"I thought you were going to join the spirit world!" said Aqiwo, relieved.

The young monk picked up a jade tray with a white pewter teapot and cup on it and knelt next to Oona.

"Grapefruit flower," he declared, as if reciting a poem.

Oona sat up and drank a few sips of the steaming liquid. She could feel a mysterious power flowing through her body, infusing it with sparks of joy.

The young monk brought a vegetarian meal consisting of white rice and bamboo shoots with soy milk, served in golden bowls.

"Eat. You need to regain your strength," Master Wada said. "An ancient Prophecy predicted the arrival of three young people, the Guardians of the Earth, capable of restoring harmony with nature and saving the planet. The Chosen One must dispel the shadows from the Pearl of Hope while driving away their own sadness. Passing this test provides access to the Second Key. Only then can the Guardians find the Supreme Crystal."

"Venerable Wada," Aqiwo mumbled between two spoonfuls of rice, "do you mean Oona has passed the Pearl of Hope test?"

But, before the Elder had time to respond …

"Look! The design on my arm has changed!" Oona exclaimed in amazement.

A series of three letters from an unknown alphabet sparkled on her skin.

"The Second Key!" laughed Master Wada.

"What is it for?" asked Oona breathlessly.

"It confers access to the Supreme Knowledge, which is preserved in the Celestial Library of Eternity," the nun disclosed with a smile.

"What do the letters mean?" asked Aqiwo.

"I don't know. This is the first time I've seen this kind of writing," confessed Master Wada, whose voice mixed with the sacred melodies sung by the monks. "The Prophecy speaks of a gem of a thousand virtues that is guarded closely in the Celestial Library."

"The Supreme Crystal …" Oona deduced.

The nun responded by laughing and clapping her hands. Nawal approached and squinted at the inscriptions. The strange letters looked like golden branches.

"It's a mixture of the abjad alphabet and Devanagari writing," she said. "This language is very rare, an ancient form of Hebrew and Sanskrit. Each of these alphabets bears an uncanny resemblance to the mathematical structure of the universe. Like Pi. This is what it says: *Om tarapatha naka* …. It means 'Follow the sky and it will show you the secret of the cosmos.'"

"'Follow the sky?'" Aqiwo repeated.

Oona and Aqiwo stared at the patterns with a puzzled look.

"I translated it as best I could," the girl said, defensively.

Just then, Oona saw a comet through the window. It vanished behind a mountain, leaving a trail of glittering dust in its wake.

"Look, a shooting star in broad daylight!" she exclaimed.

"The Prophecy is coming true," the nun exclaimed. "It predicted that a star would guide the three young people to their salvation, and that only the Chosen One would be able to activate the crystal."

Master Wada grabbed a copper spyglass and pointed it toward the mountain.

"What's over there?" asked Aqiwo, pointing to a jungle-covered crag shrouded in mist.

"That's the Mountain of the Moon," the old woman intoned.

"So that's where the Third Key is?" Nawal asked.

"Indeed, all the signs point to it being there," Wada declared.

"Let's hurry and get there before Asura beats us to it!" Aqiwo urged.

"Ah, but this mountain is an optical illusion," the nun explained, smiling broadly. "Some even say that any intruder who attempts to climb the mountain actually disappears into an abyss," she warned, putting down her spyglass. "Nobody has ever succeeded in passing through the door of the Three Bridges! I mean, nobody!" she added, forcefully.

"What is the door of the Three Bridges?" asked Oona, worried.

The Elder crinkled her eyes, laughing.

"The mountain tests the travelers' self-esteem. Three bridges lead to the heart of the mountain but only one of them is real. The other two are pure optical illusions. Yet the real bridge will also vanish if you start to doubt yourself."

"Encouraging," Oona retorted sarcastically as she stared at the smile etched into Master Wada's face, wondering if she ever got sad or upset. "Master Wada, could you tell us the rest of the Prophecy?"

The nun bowed her head, looking thoughtful.

"Oona, you must learn the art of patience. Eterna will reveal the rest of the Prophecy to you in due time."

Oona frowned, her curiosity piqued. Master Wada had dodged her question just as the goddess had cut her explanation about the Prophecy short. What else was she going to discover?

"And how will I know which bridge to choose?" she sighed.

"You will have to listen to your inner voice and trust it completely. But you need to rest first. Tomorrow, I'll teach you how to meditate. This will increase your powers. The following day, you must leave at sunrise," Wada said, before turning her back on them and disappearing behind a massive gold door.

Soon, Oona would have to overcome her doubts. The very thought of it made her quake with apprehension. Then a smile came to her lips as she thought about how she'd managed to overcome her sadness. And Aqiwo had told her that he … "loved her just as she was"! The recollection made her heart flutter like a thousand butterflies.

CHAPTER XVI
The Key to Inner Peace

The next morning, Oona was standing beside Master Wada at the entrance to the Shaolin Temple. The dawn cast amber shadows across the valley floor and the celestial bells were ringing in the distance.

"Follow me," the Elder commanded.

A gleaming shrine stood at the end of the main path, which was lined with blossoming cherry trees that filled the air with their delicate scent. Oona watched in wonder as tigers roamed freely in the courtyard among the porcupines, giant salamanders, golden pheasants, and snub-nosed monkeys. In the lush garden to her left, monks were training in martial arts, doing what looked like kung fu movements, but in slow motion.

"This is tai chi," Master Wada explained, anticipating Oona's question. "It's a martial art, like kung fu, designed to galvanize your life force, your energy. To increase your power. But it is also a philosophy of life," she added.

A monk jumped nimbly, made a few graceful kicks in the air, and fell gently to his knees. Watching him, Oona realized she still had a long way to go!

"Don't forget to practice the Needle at Sea Bottom," the nun told the fighter. "It's one of the most difficult postures to do perfectly," she explained to Oona before adding with a laugh, "He's been trying for sixteen years. Kung fu warriors never give up!"

The monks smiled at them warmly as they passed by. To their right, young monks were breaking bricks with their heads.

"Kung fu requires years of hard training. Martial artists learn to discipline both their minds and their bodies," Master Wada explained.

Then she stopped in front of a gigantic statue of an elephant that was lying on its side in the middle of a patch of green grass.

"Lift it up," ordered the Master.

"Excuse me?" Oona asked, surprised.

"Lift it up," the nun repeated with a wide grin.

"I might be able to light a torch but … that? That would be a miracle!" exclaimed Oona, shaking her head.

Master Wada pointed to the sun and the pale disk of the moon, both visible high in the azure sky.

"And these perfectly round celestial beings hanging in the sky? Don't you think that's a miracle?"

Oona looked at the sun and the moon floating side by side and smiled. Master Wada had a point: the starry sky was indeed a real miracle. The Earth too … Then she turned her attention back to the statue, squinted, and let out an angry snarl as she stretched her hands out toward the stone elephant. Beads of sweat dampened her forehead. At last, a spark of energy shot out from her clammy palms, but the elephant didn't budge an inch.

"You see, the problem is that you don't believe enough in yourself, and therefore you also doubt your powers. Everything is possible, Oona," the Elder said. Then, suddenly: "Free yourself!" she bellowed.

Oona took a deep breath. *I can do it; I can do it …* she repeated to herself with complete conviction. The spark grew and a wave of bluish particles washed over the elephant.

"Stay calm. Let your emotions flow like a river. You are the captain of your ship. The mind is limitless," the nun asserted.

The statue rose into the air, then appeared to simply hang there. Then, with a resounding thud, the huge elephant fell heavily on its side.

"Almost. Next time, without your hands," Master Wada laughed, righting the elephant with the back of her kimono sleeve. Then she sat on the ground and pointed to Nawal and Aqiwo, who were sitting in the lotus position beneath a cherry tree in bloom, their eyes closed, while the statue tottered, then fell back on the ground on its other side. Master Wada's mental force was too strong!

"The nature of birds is to sing," Wada declared. "In meditation, humans access their true nature, which is love, and the source of all power. They go back to being like the birds, chattering in the trees."

She gestured to Oona to come and sit next to her.

"And now? What should I do?" Oona asked excitedly.

"You'll see, it's easy. Close your eyes and breathe in deeply. Then, exhale and relax your entire body."

Oona did as Master Wada said and exhaled loudly.

"There, that's good. Now, whenever you think of something, repeat the word 'Eterna' in your mind."

"And then?

"That's all."

"That's all? I just need to close my eyes and repeat 'Eterna' whenever I think of something?"

"That's right."

"Is it to keep me from thinking?" Oona noticed that her thoughts were like a barrier reef she had to cross to reach an ocean of peace!

"It's not possible to stop thinking, but you can observe your thoughts as though they were sheep passing by. And repeating the word 'Eterna' is one way, a kind of key, to open the door to that inner garden of serenity, that's sheltered from the storms of the outside world. Go ahead, close your eyes and give it a try."

Oona followed the master's instructions, allowing her eyelids to droop and breathing deeply. Immediately, she thought of Aqiwo. He seemed to have been avoiding her gaze since his emotional outpouring the day before. Aha, a thought! *Eterna, Eterna, Eterna ...* Oona noticed that repeating the word distracted her from her thoughts. A wave of well-being coursed through her body, sending delicious shivers through her limbs. After a few minutes, Oona couldn't resist opening an eye. Master Wada was floating beside her in a halo of unearthly light, levitating. She widened her eyes, astounded. Strangely enough, hours – not minutes – must have passed because they were alone in the garden and the air had turned cool. The sun was vanishing behind the Mountain of the Moon and the first stars were lighting up the mauve sky. Oona's gaze fell on the elephant statue lying in the grass a few yards away, its grey rock eyes seeming to plead for help. Without a second thought, she focused all her mental energy on the statue, which suddenly rose up into the air, its stone trunk lifted toward the moon. Oona's mouth gaped in amazement. In the dark night, she shed a secret tear of happiness.

***

At dawn, Master Wada and the young monk were standing in front of the monastery gate, holding rice paper lanterns.

"Goodbye, Venerable Wada," said Oona with a bow. "I thank you very much. I will try not to forget your lessons."

She couldn't hold back the tears that welled up in her eyes. Oona had been moved by the nun's immense wisdom and felt deeply attached to her. Nawal and Aqiwo also bowed sadly.

"Remember, valiant Guardian of Earth. Don't doubt yourself," Master Wada urged, placing her hand on Oona's shoulder.

For once, the Elder wasn't laughing. In fact, her eyes were wet with tears. Oona raised her head, sniffling. Moon Mountain's enormous peak stood out against the sky, casting its enormous shadow over the peaceful monastery.

CHAPTER XVII
The Three Bridges

The next morning, the Guardians walked to the edge of the forest. The glowing disc of the Sun cast an orangish halo on the mountain covered with countless white flowers. Oona was on high alert, carefully surveying their surroundings. Peering at the ground, she thought she saw jade-colored plants raising their heads with every step they took, as if watching them. The verdant pines and tall bamboo moved constantly in the wind, quivering like a swarm of dragonflies.

As the Guardians made their way through the vegetation, the trees gradually took on a bluish tone, as if the trio had passed through an invisible wall that led to another dimension. They were following a narrow path illuminated by the Sun when, suddenly, the trees vanished and a meadow appeared before their eyes. The wind was blowing dandelion seeds across the lush grass and white, cottony clouds were dancing around them.

"It's like snow!" exclaimed Nawal.

"They're dandelion seeds, the flower of the stars!" Aqiwo said in admiration.

Oona reached out to catch one of the fluffy seeds swirling in the breeze.

"Aqiwo, why do you call them 'flowers of the stars'?" she asked.

"The yellow flower looks like the Sun, the puff looks like the Moon, and the seeds sown by the wind look like stars," he explained.

"The Second Key told us to follow the stars," said Oona, staring at the pattern on her arm.

"Do you think this means we're on the right path?" asked Aqiwo.

"Look!" interjected Nawal.

Three huge stone bridges loomed before them, their far ends hidden in a mass of clouds. Three bridges toward infinity, suspended in the sky. The Guardians let out a cry of surprise. Curious, Oona approached the nearest bridge and leaned over the guardrail. Her stomach churned at the terrifying sight of a bottomless ravine. Suddenly, she felt very small.

"Yikes!" exclaimed Aqiwo, staring at the precipice. "Maybe it's better if I go first. What do you think?"

Oona was touched by Aqiwo's concern, but her sense of duty came first. She had to accomplish the mission she'd been assigned.

"No, Aqiwo, that's kind of you, but you heard the Prophecy," she replied.

"But how are you going to know which bridge to cross?" he persisted.

"Don't worry, Master Wada taught me to meditate."

Oona moved away from the first bridge and stood in front of the three structures.

"Good luck, Oona!" Nawal called out, her fists clenched.

Oona closed her eyes, then filled her lungs with air and relaxed her entire body. *Eterna, Eterna, Eterna …* he repeated, as her mentor had instructed her. Waves of the word surged through her mind, chasing away all other thoughts. Finally, it felt as if there were a cool wind and calm water inside her head. She opened her eyes and looked carefully at each of the bridges. The one on her far right seemed to be surrounded by a whitish halo, which drew her irresistibly. The nun had told her to trust her inner voice, so she took a step toward it.

"I can't watch!" Nawal murmured, hiding her eyes.

Oona breathed in deeply and prepared to step onto on the span. She'd been afraid of heights her whole life, and now she had a life-and-death mission that involved walking on floating bridges suspended over an abyss! While tempted to smile at the irony of it, her terror at the prospect of falling prevented her from actually doing so. Placing her right foot gingerly on the bridge, she swung the other foot forward so all her weight was on the bridge. Disconcertingly, Oona only felt emptiness under the sole of her foot, which felt around in the void. She swallowed, her throat dry with anxiety as vertigo clouded her thoughts. *Eterna, Eterna, Eterna …* she kept repeating softly to herself, like a serenade. Suddenly, a hard surface materialized beneath her foot, allowing her to support the weight of her body on the structure that was taking shape through her mental effort. She took yet another step, attempting to concentrate on the cool calm inside her head, to prevent any doubt from entering her mind.

"Keep going, Oona!" Aqiwo urged.

Oona stared straight ahead without batting an eyelid, as if sustained by a supernatural force. Slowly, rhythmically, taking one step after another, she advanced on the stone bridge that was materializing because of her belief in herself. Ahead of her, the mass of fluffy clouds was turning into an impenetrable fog that was drawing ever closer and obscuring the end of the bridge. What could be on the other side? Hesitatingly, she ventured near the parapet and leaned over. The bottom of the precipice was veiled by opaque, whitish wisps but then, suddenly, a shape caught her eye and filled her with a sense of dread. Oona fought against the vertigo that gripped her and leaned her chest against the stone wall to see it better. It was the body of a person or large animal that had washed up on the rocky shore at the bottom of the chasm. This was the fate that awaited her if she was unable to control her mind!

"Oona, don't stop!" Aqiwo called out. "Don't look down. It's probably a trap, and it's too late to go back anyway!"

Immediately, Oona pulled back and started to repeat *Eterna* again, before any fear or doubt could take shape in her mind. She had just resumed her confident course when she heard a voice behind her:

"You'll never make it!"

Oona's blood ran cold as she recognized the all-too-familiar voice that always took the wind out of her sails.

"Daddy?!" she cried, whirling around, terrified.

Her father was standing between Nawal and Aqiwo with a sadistic sneer on his lips. Her friends had leaped backwards and assumed defensive positions.

"I mean, look at yourself. How could you even imagine that you're the Chosen One? That you're special?" he jeered.

His words pierced Oona's heart like a sharp blade.

"How dare you?" said Aqiwo indignantly. "Shut up!"

Oona stared at her father: his wickedness showed clearly in his eyes and on his face, giving him a hideous expression. Her pulse quickened with fear and she felt her resolve weaken as tears welled up in her eyes. A dull roar was rising in the air, accompanied by clouds of dust as the bridge began to shake.

"NO! Don't doubt, Oona! Don't listen to him! Don't doubt!" Aqiwo shouted urgently.

Oona bit her lip as Nawal closed her eyes. Furious, she turned around to continue her progress, fighting with all her mental power against that devastating voice and the self-doubt it created. She tightened her jaw and tried to strengthen her resolve. She had to focus! *Eterna, Eterna, Eterna …* Still, her concentration was clouded by the questions flooding her mind. How did he know she was the Chosen One? And, more importantly, what was he doing here?

A huge chunk of rock crumbled and fell heavily into the void, interrupting her thoughts. She clenched her fists but couldn't help but turn around to face her father once again. She shivered, terrified, as her father's face changed before her eyes to assume the features of her cosmic enemy.

"ASURA?!" she cried, horrified.

What was happening? Had Asura taken on her father's appearance to make her doubt? Were her senses playing tricks on her?

"You ... you're my father?" she stammered, petrified.

"Let's just say I took your father's place on Earth a few years ago," he replied with a sneer.

Oona's mind reeled with the shock, and she felt her legs swaying as vertigo overtook her. What was he talking about? This didn't make any sense!

"Who is my father, then?" she queried, incredulous.

"So, you don't know?" he laughed. "Balthazar isn't your real father. I took over his appearance years ago so that I could keep an eye on you."

Oona shuddered with revulsion. Sickened, she looked at Asura's monstrous face as her thoughts churned. Then, gathering all her mental strength, she turned away and again began repeating her mantra: *Eterna, Eterna, Eterna...* She clung to the magic word like a castaway clings to a life preserver, then dashed toward the end of the bridge, still obscured by clouds. The bridge cracked and boulders shot out from all sides like a volcano spewing rocks. The stones of the bridge scarcely supported her steps, crumbling as soon as she put her foot on them, pulverized by the tremors of the edifice which collapsed behind her. Still, she ran, desperate, with Asura's demonic laughter echoing behind her as a multitude of multicolored birds took flight, setting the restless sky ablaze. *Eterna, Eterna,*

Eterna … The clouds converged around the summit of Moon Mountain in a tempestuous whirlwind. The dark swirls contrasted with the sky that was clearing in her mind as she meditated. Finally, her mind was filled with indescribable brightness, and she felt a wondrous power awakening in her body, flickering in every one of her cells. An explosion of light radiated through her entire being. Oona stopped dead in her tracks, then turned around. She had the feeling that this tremendous, force was guiding her body, making her invincible.

"Your words don't have any power over me any-more!" she declared forcefully, glaring at Asura.

The shaking of the bridge subsided. Asura looked taken aback, then clenched his fists.

"I can do this, you'll see!" she challenged.

As soon as she said these words, the bridge stopped collapsing. Oona was now more than twenty yards from the far side on the half-destroyed bridge, leaving half of it cut off in midair. Nawal and Aqiwo had entered their respective bubbles and started rolling huge rocks from the mountain toward Asura. Asura dodged the boulders, and the two Guardians took advantage of their target's distraction to float toward Oona. Glancing behind her toward where the bridge reached down into the clouds, she saw that a luminous passage drenched in golden light had opened up amid the billowy mass. She'd done it!

CHAPTER XVIII
The Celestial Library

Nawal and Aqiwo's bubbles vanished and, together, the three Guardians walked slowly toward the bright light like moths drawn to a flame. Alongside them there suddenly appeared endless shelves of books supported by immense concave crystal walls. Then, an avenue of white marble columns leading into the egg-shaped building materialized before their astonished eyes.

"What is …?" asked Aqiwo.

"The Celestial Library … It's incredible!" Oona answered, amazed.

"Do you think there's something special about these books?" he wondered.

"All books are special!" Oona said firmly. "According to the one I have on ancient Egypt, this library contains all the books humans have ever written. The collection of all learning, the sanctuary of universal knowledge," she enthused, looking reverently at the spines of the volumes.

She felt like she was in heaven. Books had always been her family and her refuge, enabling her to read about the adventures of heroes who were even worse off than she was, to dream of extraordinary destinies, to discover worlds inhabited by marvelous characters. Abruptly, the columns stopped and an inner courtyard with a beautiful garden lay before them. Aqiwo walked toward a patch of pearl-colored grass that glowed faintly with an iridescent light. Nawal and Oona exchanged a look and followed him. Glittering lotus flowers bloomed at their feet in a fantastic variety of pastel colors.

Oona felt a feather brush her cheek. Tiny turquoise birds were flying around them, tickling them with their wings and twirling joyfully in the air. Then, to her amazement, red and purple letters began floating before her eyes, as if they had somehow escaped from the books, and the air turned a gorgeous shade of green-ish-blue, with bursts of brilliant cyan blue glittering around them.

Oona had the feeling that they were the lead dancers in a cosmic ballet above a luminous, ever-changing garden of Eden.

In the center of the garden, above an altar drenched in light, a small crystal floated, its four sides decorated with constellations.

"Look," Aqiwo whispered.

Oona's heart stopped for an instant and Nawal kept silent, as if enchanted by this vision in stone. The three Guardians were both dazzled and deeply moved.

"The Supreme Crystal …" Oona whispered.

"A stone that has the beauty of Earth, the purity of Heaven, the power of the Sun, and the sacred brilliance of the Moon. It has been under the influence of the celestial bodies for so long that it contains all the powers of the cosmos," Nawal proclaimed.

At these words, Oona looked up … and bit back an exclamation of surprise. A wide slit at the top of the crystal had just opened, like a window to the sky. The solar eclipse had begun, and the Moon was orbiting resolutely toward the Sun.

"The eclipse! We must hurry, or it'll be too late to activate the crystal!"

Nawal and Aqiwo looked up.

"Look, Astera is here!" Aqiwo announced, pointing to the Supreme Crystal.

Oona saw the Dark Planet's immense lava eyes hovering over the altar before they suddenly vanished.

"Where?" asked Nawal.

"I saw his eyes over the altar!" Oona asserted, rushing to the pedestal to seize the crystal.

She was just about to seize the supreme stone when her hand crashed into an invisible barrier; the jewel was surrounded by a slim but impenetrable wall. Oona winced as she rubbed her sore hand. She felt around on all sides but there was no doubt about it: a kind of mysterious casing protected the crystal.

"'I can't get to it, it's like there's an invisible wall!" she wailed.

Looking down, she saw three shooting stars pointing to three golden planets engraved into the ground.

"Follow the sky, follow the sky," Oona chanted in a hushed voice. "Just like Nawal said. Let's stand on the planets, maybe we're the Third key!"

The Guardians dashed forward and stood on the other two engravings in front of the Supreme Crystal.

"And now?" asked Nawal.

Suddenly, the Supreme Crystal levitated and spun in the air, emitting three blinding rays of purple light. Oona reached her hand out to grasp the jewel. The invisible barrier had disappeared! Just then, a white eagle flew through the opening into the sanctuary and circled in the air before landing among the three Guardians and resuming his human form.

"Thothan!" cried Oona. While thrilled to see him, she had no time to lose, and rushed toward the altar.

A swan-shaped cloud appeared in the sky above them, which parted to reveal Eterna, slumped over in her celestial chariot. She slowly raised her head, which was crowned with sprigs of lily-of-the-valley, and it seemed to cost her a great effort to speak.

"You have found the Supreme Crystal, *min tolthi*," she said in an almost inaudible voice, moving her lips made of raspberries.

Suddenly, Astera materialized before the Guardians, and Oona took a hasty step backwards. The massive goddess was draped in shadows and from her glowing hair, red-hot ashes flew into the air.

"Yes, Eterna, and the time for my reign has finally come!" she roared. "Did you really think you could get rid of me that easily? That you could betray me without suffering the consequences?"

"You left me no choice," countered Eterna, with a burst of energy. "You are the one who betrayed Life by harnessing light to satisfy your own insatiable thirst for power!" she thundered in a mighty voice that expressed all of Nature's might.

Earth's spirit was standing as tall as a mountain, her eyes glowing with cold rage. Her maternal instinct toward her earthly children seemed to have suddenly revived her.

"How dare you?" boomed the Dark Planet. "How could you forget the thousands of years of friendship between us? How could you put me in a black hole, after I saved your life?" she hollered indignantly, spewing lava. "May all the powers of the Earth and the Milky Way be mine!"

She pointed her finger imperiously at the spinning jewel.

"Asura, seize the Supreme Crystal!"

The evil goddess burst into flames, sending snake-like coils of ash all around her as Asura emerged from behind the pillar where he had been skulking.

"Watch out, Oona! Behind you!" Nawal yelled.

Oona turned around and screamed in horror, recoiling from the sight of Asura as her forehead and palms blazed with scarlet light. The avatar walked menacingly toward Oona, accompanied by the little pig she'd seen in a dream what seemed like a lifetime ago, now a colossal wild boar. His sharp tusks were pointing in the air like two deadly harpoons.

The crimson wave of light grew and grew as anger surged inside her, expressing the fury she felt toward her longtime foe. Asura! He had dared to take on the role of her father and then torment and belittle her! She jumped into the air, grabbed the spinning gem, and swooped down behind the crystal pedestal, the fire of her anger setting the foliage in her path ablaze.

Breathless, she held the precious crystal delicately in her hands.

Meanwhile, Aqiwo jumped valiantly in front of the boar, blocking his path.

"Give the gem back, Oona!" Asura commanded, brandishing a gigantic sword. "It's too late to save Eterna now."

The terrifying blade was slicing the air above Oona's head.

"Give me the crystal," he barked, glowering.

Oona clutched the Supreme Crystal to her chest.

"Never!" she exclaimed.

Glancing around, she realized the wild boar was about to charge Aqiwo, who was staring him down.

"Aqiwo!" she shouted.

As Aqiwo's gaze locked with the boar's, his eyes grew wide in astonishment. The fierce beast, however, stopped dead in his tracks.

Oona grimaced in pain, as if she'd been punched in the stomach. Looking at the boar, she realized she could feel the animal's emotions: he had seen his entire life story in Aqiwo's eyes, like a mirror of truth. Her throat tightened in sympathy as the boar discovered the truth about his past. She saw what the beast saw: Asura capturing his parents, just like in her dream! The boar was overcome with confusion and horror, which Oona could also feel, like a weight in her chest. He had pretended to save him in the forest, but Asura the one who was responsible for all his troubles! The double betrayal caused the animal – and Oona – great pain. Letting out a long, mournful wail, he spun around and narrowed its eyes in anger, seeming to search for Asura.

Just visible through the gap in the ceiling, Oona could see the Moon approaching the Sun, about to eclipse it.

Thothan and Nawal threw themselves at Asura, who swept his attackers away with the back of his arm, making them fly to the other side of the courtyard. Then he drew his bow and rained an onslaught of arrows down on them. The two Guardians held their palms up, their energy stopping each arrow in its tracks. Meanwhile, Astera's shadow was towering over Oona.

The dark deity suddenly turned into a hideous dragon and Oona let out a shrill cry. She remembered the Prophecy, where she'd seen herself brandishing a crystal while a dragon stared menacingly down at her! The entire altar was hidden by the expanse of the monster's wings. The horrifying creature shook its reptilian head and lowered it toward Oona, who closed her eyes and clutched the gem firmly to her chest. Her chin was shaking. Astera let out a terrifying hiss, threw her head back, and opened her enormous jaws a few inches from Oona's face. She felt herself swaying with fear, her blood running cold. She took a step backwards, tripped, and fell to the ground. Was this the end?

CHAPTER XIX
The Filaments of Light

A ray of light struck Astera's dragon eyes, blinding her. She closed them and shook her head violently. Oona held her breath, petrified. Her ears were ringing, and her limbs were paralyzed with fear. Finally, the dragon straightened her head, her pupils seeming to narrow in anger and pain. Oona followed its piercing gaze. Comets were shooting out from the Sun to create a ring of glowing lights around the Moon. Incredible! The string of meteors prevented the Moon from advancing further, blocking its path toward the Sun.

Eterna was fading, barely conscious in her celestial carriage, but a glimmer of love shone dimly in her half-open eyes.

"Ra …" she murmured, gratefully.

"Ra is delaying the eclipse!" Nawal exclaimed.

Astera raised her monstrous head toward the sky and roared.

"The Sun is holding back the Moon in order to save Eterna," Aqiwo added, fascinated.

The Moon, in turn was emitting balls of blue light to fight against the Sun's burning halo.

Eterna spoke. "My children, Ra will not be able to restrain the Moon for long, since it controls the tides throughout the Milky Way, and delaying it would disturb the lives of other celestial beings."

Blinded by the light from the Sun, Astera moved her head uncontrollably back and forth while her tail whipping the air in all directions. Oona remained vigilant, ready to jump out of the way. On the other side of the altar, she saw the boar charging Asura. Then the dragon's tail whacked Thothan, who fell to the ground.

"Thothan!" Oona shouted in dismay.

A stream of gold flowed from his body and spread across the ground as he gradually regained his eagle form. Despite the tragedy of the situation, she couldn't help but think, *The demigod's veins run with gold?* The sword-like tip of Astera's tail was swinging above him, ready to finish him off with a stab to the heart. Oona shuddered with fright, unable to move, but Nawal rushed to the wounded bird and pulled him aside just in time. Oona heaved a sigh of relief, then leapt to her feet. Her blood was boiling. She remained still for a moment, then lifted her chin, her eyes flashing with unyielding determination. Her fear had completely vanished.

"You want to fight? Then let's fight!" she shouted, giving her enemy a death stare.

Astera looked up, surprised by Oona's challenge. In response, she threw back her immense head and spewed a jet of flames in her direction. But Oona jumped in the air and landed on top of the dragon's head, which shook violently in an attempt to dislodge her. Oona staggered and started to slide, clutching frantically at Astera's scales, but ended up falling. Blood-red flames came out of the creature's mouth, spreading in all directions like the tentacles of an enraged octopus. Lying on the ground, Oona felt the sting of a burning slap on her ankle and cringed in pain. The blades of fire danced before her, their heat scorching her face. She squinted and focused with all her might, reaching her hands to the sky for help. Oona struggled with her fear as the flames devoured everything in their path, leaving nothing but charred devastation in their wake.

Suddenly, a large white "V" took shape in the sky. Oona's face broke into a grin and her heart beat wildly. Her call had been heard! Then the formation exploded into a flock of Dalmatian pelicans that scattered over the sky, the large pouches of their long yellow beaks swaying heavily. The white and grey-speckled birds descended upon Astera and opened their beaks, releasing torrential downpours that immediately extinguished the flames. Oona felt like clapping! The pelicans tilted their heads toward her as if in salute, then flew through the opening back up into the sky, their wings flapping loudly.

Next, her attention was caught by Aqiwo, who was busy evading Asura's arrows. Her stomach tied in knots as she saw him leap over the avatar's head, then land in a puddle behind him. Asura turned and struck hard in the direction of Aqiwo's chest. Oona's jaw tensed. But her friend pulled back, avoiding the blow, and twirled in the air like a dancer. *Good job, Aqiwo!* Oona then noticed the boar charging Asura, snarling furiously. She held her breath as Asura ran in the opposite direction. The beast chased after him and then, at the stairs leading to the altar, slammed into him, knocking him onto the glass steps, which were covered in water from the pelican's rescue. Aqiwo took advantage of the situation to jump on Asura's chest and pin his shoulders down with his knees. He let out a long kung fu battle cry, then pressed down with his thumb between his victim's eyebrows.

"Arghhhhhh!" Asura groaned under the lethal pressure.

But Astera swooped down on Aqiwo and tore him away from his opponent.

"Aqiwo! No!!!" screamed Oona as she desperately reached her arms toward the roaring monster. "Leave him alone!"

"Give me the gem!" Astera commanded as she waved Aqiwo in front of Oona.

Her friend was writhing in all directions, trying to push back the scaly talons that were clutching him.

"Never!" Oona retorted, fuming with anger.

"As you like," the reptile hissed as she brought Aqiwo up to the chasm of her enormous mouth.

The young boy let out a cry of terror that tore through Oona's insides. What should she do? She couldn't give up on him! But handing the Supreme Crystal over to Astera would mean the downfall of Eterna, the destruction of Earth, and the extinction of all humans! Her brain, plagued by a thousand conflicting thoughts, was tortured by the sound of Aqiwo's cries. In the blink of an eye, her mind conjured up images of her friend's laughing face, the memory of his hand in hers, and the warmth of his compassionate gaze.

"Stop it! Okay, I give up … I'm begging you, don't hurt him!" she implored, sweating profusely.

The sinister deity responded to Oona's surrender with a demonic laugh.

"No, Oona!" protested Aqiwo, still wriggling in all directions and pushing on the monster's talons to free himself from their grip.

"Don't! Think of Eterna! Think of the Earth!"

Oona stared at the glittering gem and then at the sky. The solar eclipse was almost complete, and the pelicans were circling in the air, as if awaiting her instructions. Her vision blurred with tears. Choosing between Aqiwo and Eterna was like having her heart torn in two! Sweat ran down her back. She took a step forward. She couldn't sacrifice Aqiwo!

"Oona, no! I'm begging you!"

Ignoring her friend's pleas, she walked defeatedly toward the dragon.

"We could all live in peace," she implored, clutching the Supreme Crystal to her chest. "Eterna could teach you about the beauty of life."

"Give me the gem! *I* will live in peace for eternity!" thundered Astera, her eyes burning with greed.

The dragon pawed at her, her talons grazing the Supreme Crystal. Suddenly, Oona had an idea. Taking a deep breath to clear her head, she gathered all her mental strength as a wave of power surged through her. Then she closed her eyes for a moment. Suddenly, legions of bees rose from the sacred garden in black, buzzing columns. With a resounding roar, the swarms arranged themselves into attack formation and raced toward Astera, attacking her from all sides. Taken aback, the monster shook her huge head and swung her scaly tail in the air. Oona redoubled her efforts, then threw one of her hands forward, like a conductor's baton, to guide the humming battalions. The bees continued tormenting the monster, surrounding her head in a dark, buzzing cloud. Astera let out a long, harrowing wail and released her grip. Aqiwo fell to the ground, spared by the army of winged allies.

"Aqiwo!" screamed Oona as she rushed toward him.

He stopped her in her tracks with a wave of his hand.

"Quickly, Oona, the eclipse!" replied Aqiwo, pointing to the sky.

Oona saw Eterna above her and her thoughts moved at lightning speed. She rushed to Thothan, who was bathed in a pool of gold. With a burst of energy, he managed to get back on his feet and motioned Oona to climb onto his silky neck. The great white bird began to glow as soon as the Supreme Crystal touched his feathers and, rising into the air, flew toward Eterna. Oona felt her heart beat with excitement. She was just a few inches from the goddess who was lying in her celestial chariot, smiling weakly up at her. Feverish, Oona deposited the sacred gem into her cupped hands. Her heart was beating wildly. Then she noticed that her hands, like Tothan's feathers, were now glowing. What was happening to her?

"*Min tolthae*, you did it …" the Earth spirit murmured, as tears filled her large, aquamarine eyes.

Beads of pearly foam hung on the dill fronds of her eyelashes.

Eterna carefully took the small crystal, now a pyramid bejeweled with stars, in her fingers of coral. Oona held her breath, captivated. Then the goddess placed the sacred gem on her heart, which immediately blossomed in an explosion of light. The release was so powerful that Thothan and Oona were thrown to the ground. Thunder rumbled in the miraculous garden, and the bed of moss she'd landed on was shaking. What was going on? Oona looked up, shielding her eyes with her hand. Beneath her fingers, she could see the sky gradually illuminated as myriads of burgeoning stars burst forth. A dazzling light shot through the air around them, though she was still able to discern Astera blinking and shrieking nearby, her eyelids so swollen by bee stings that she could scarcely see. Then Eterna's angelic face filled the sky.

Her marvelous beauty had been restored, and her cheeks, glowing pink with rose petals, were framed by dangling locks of lavender. The sumptuous goddess was draped in orchids, meadowsweet, daffodils, cornflowers, and daisies, and the Supreme Crystal lay in majesty in her heart of crimson poppies, once again beating to the rhythm of Earth. Oona sighed with wonder. Astera roared furiously, emitting a deafening wail. Oona saw her swing her tail in Aqiwo's direction, sweeping away everything in its path.

"Aqiwo! No!!" shouted Oona.

Too late! He was hurtled into the air and fell face-down a few yards away. Oona rushed toward him, but Astera beat her to it, driving the sharp end of her tail in the young boy's back. Oona felt like the ground was giving way under her feet. A red spot appeared on her friend's amber-colored tunic, then grew larger. A trickle of scarlet ran onto the ground.

"Aqiwo!" Oona screamed again.

He let out a piercing cry, like the shrill yelp of a wounded animal. In the middle of the garden, a geyser of light was making its way through the trees. Oona moved back despite herself. A cloud of phosphorescent butterflies flew from the marvelous garden toward the stars. She heard Asura groan and gave him a vindictive look. His face was starting to melt, gradually liquefying into a coal-black puddle beneath the empty shell of his armor. Astera bellowed, this time probably out of fear. An enormous black hole opened above her reptilian head. The evil creature screeched as she was whirled away and swallowed by a black hole. Reduced to nothing, her destruction set the sky ablaze. Finally, Oona ran to Aqiwo, turned him over and hugged him, her heart in her mouth. His eyes were closed, and he was struggling to breathe, his limbs too weak to respond to her embrace. He was dying!

Eterna's sphere appeared near the Guardians and spun in the air. Through a curtain of tears, Oona saw shooting stars within the sphere that rained down from a sunless, darkened sky. Long filaments of light were striking the Earth, creating little luminous points on each continent, as if lamps were being lit one by one across the globe.

Aqiwo's eyes opened wide in wonderment at the vision of the dawn of a new Earth dancing before him.

"Aqiwo!" Oona implored. "Hold on! Stay with us … I … I need you!"

"Oona, help me see what's happening …" he whispered, his eyes shining.

Oona lifted her friend's head onto her lap so he could witness the spectacle taking place in Eterna's sphere.

The Sun was slowly emerging from behind the Moon, signaling a new dawn for planet Earth. Oona's eyes widened. Outraged, she saw an elephant tied to a wooden post in the middle of a field, its four legs hobbled by a rope. The noble animal was standing upright and seemed to be gazing up at the sky. Its heavy, wrinkled head had a pitifully broken tusk, as if deprived of its majesty by shameless beings. Her cheeks burned with indignation. A hunter approached, rifle in hand. Oona wanted to jump up and join the animal in the sphere in order to set it free. Then the man blinked. The dark light that obscured his eyes dissipated, revealing the continents of the Earth. Oona let out a cry of astonishment. The hunter dropped his rifle on the grass and ran toward the elephant. What was he going to do? To her great surprise, the hunter put his hand on the animal's cracked forehead then hastened to untie it. Oona laughed in stupefaction, but then stopped herself, redirecting her attention to Aqiwo. A peaceful smile hovered on her friend's lips.

"Eterna is saved," he murmured.

At these words, a part of Oona's heart leapt with happiness. She loved the Earth so much. The young boy's face lit up with a golden light, radiating infinite peace. Oona could see the image of his parents and his grandmother in his irises, walking toward him in a cocoon of light. Oona felt as if her heart were split in two. She felt immense fulfilment, but also infinite sorrow at the idea of losing her friend.

"Oona, remember, you will never be alone," he said, smiling.

Tears of despair flooded Oona's eyes as Aqiwo's eyelids closed like the curtains at the end of a play.

"No! Noooo!"

Furiously, Oona pounded Aqiwo's chest, then collapsed on him, sobbing, an indescribable pain piercing her heart like a knife.

CHAPTER XX
The Key to Life

Eterna floated above the Guardians, her face made of roses filling the clear sky. Thothan brushed her enormous, coral cheeks with his glittering wings and landed on the branch of a tree in the forest of her hair. Within the sphere, Oona saw billions of tiny light filaments connecting to the goddess's poppy-red heart. The luminous threads were once again connected to the humans' hearts. Despite her overwhelming sorrow, Oona sighed in wonder. The goddess descended from the firmament toward Oona and Nawal and resumed her human form, the white eagle perched on her graceful shoulder. Her hair shone with a pearly brightness.

"Eterna, Aqiwo is dead!" Oona howled, tears streaming down her cheeks.

Nawal was holding her hand. She and Oona were both sitting at the foot of a lotus with twisted roots that splayed out from the base of the tree like melted candle wax.

"The Supreme Crystal was activated thanks to the purity of your hearts, for love is the supreme key, the key to life," Eterna said, kneeling down beside them and gazing sadly at Aqiwo. "You saved Earth and all the stars," she added, her eyes exuding infinite gratitude.

The goddess embraced Oona and stroked her hair. The girl collapsed in her arms, sobbing inconsolably. As soon as Oona felt her touch, a wave of well-being spread through her body and her grief gradually yielded to a serene acceptance: she felt protected, as if she was floating on a cloud of love. Nestled against Eterna's warm chest, Oona forgot everything, abandoning herself to the maternal embrace of the spirit of the Earth.

"*Min tolthae,*" the deity whispered in a voice filled with tenderness, pushing back a lock of Oona's hair. "You have the power to bring Aqiwo back to life."

"Me? Really?" Oona queried, sitting up. "Aqiwo can be saved?" she asked, again, astonished and shaken by the news.

"Yes," said Eterna. "Now is the time for me to tell you the rest of the Prophecy. But let's start at the beginning. At the beginning of time, Astera was my best friend."

Oona gave a gasp of surprise while Nawal, flabbergasted, reached out and squeezed her fingers.

"Back then, we loved each other like sisters," Eterna said, her voice tinged with nostalgia.

The sphere depicted the goddess's words like a mirror.

"Sixty-five million years ago, a gigantic asteroid struck the Earth's surface in the Yucatan state of Mexico, wiping out much of the life forms there and causing me great harm."

In the sacred ball, a velociraptor and a tyrannosaurus were staring at the sky, their eyes blank with terror. A meteorite hit the planet's surface with full force, exterminating most of the dinosaurs and animals. Eterna slumped in her celestial chariot, half-conscious, her hair singed. Oona hid her eyes with her hands.

"Astera traveled throughout the cosmos, desperately seeking help to save me."

"Astera? Really?" Nawal exclaimed, still not able to accept that the Dark Planet could once have been Earth's ally.

"Yes, Nawal. This is when the Luminous Beings came to help us. As you already know, they also have the power of light, which is the power that gives life and cures all ills. And they are the only ones in the cosmos able to create new stars in the sky."

In the ball, a slender being with translucent, bluish skin like a jellyfish, and an elongated face with two benevolent, pearl-colored eyes extended its hands skyward and placed a star there. Oona sighed with wonder. So, the Luminous Beings created the stars in the sky! Did this mean she had discovered the great secret of the Cosmos …? She couldn't believe her eyes or her ears!

"The Luminous Beings used their power to save me," Eterna continued.

In the ball, a dozen Beings were surrounding Eterna as she lay on a bed of honeysuckle, their luminous hands placed flat on her charred body, transmitting the light from their bodies to the spirit of the Earth. The light made a thousand buds blossom in her hair: daisies, forget-me-nots, and marigolds, blooming in the green vegetation of her locks. Amazed, Oona and Nawal squeezed each other's hands.

"Astera and the Luminous Beings saved me," Eterna continued. "They taught us how to use the power of light. I swore to protect their people so that new stars would always be created in the sky. Astera, however, was seduced by this power, and was only interested in using it to increase her own strength. And so, instead of giving it away, she started to absorb the light of the stars. Her first victim was her own blue sun, which she reduced to nothing by devouring all its light."

In the sphere, Astera stretched her hands out toward a blue sun. The star's intensity gradually diminished as she absorbed its light until it was completely extinguished. Her body now surrounded by a blue halo, Astera spat out her first flames. Insatiable, she was already extending her hands toward another sun, and its light also started to flicker. Oona let go of Nawal's hand and clenched her fists, aggrieved by the star's demise.

"One by one, Astera extinguished the stars in the sky. As she did so, she gradually transformed, burned by all the assimilated light."

Oona's blood boiled and she felt choked with grief. Astera had murdered stars? Those innocent luminous spheres radiating hope? With tears in her eyes, she thought of her star, her second home.

"I tried to reason with her, but to no avail. She left me no choice but to fight her. After I won, I managed to exile her to a black hole to protect the stars. I assume she felt betrayed. However, far from realizing the error of her ways, her selfish thirst for power and beauty only intensified and, along with it, her desire for revenge against me. When a white hole collided with the black hole, she took advantage of the situation and escaped."

Nawal shook her head.

"What is a white hole?" she asked.

"A white hole is the opposite of a black hole," Eterna replied. "Instead of sucking everything in, the white hole expels all matter, so anything that's imprisoned in a black hole is freed."

"And what happened after Astera escaped?" Oona asked anxiously.

"The Luminous Beings were alarmed by her actions, so they decided they had to stop her at all costs. Yet they weren't powerful enough to protect themselves from her power, which had grown strong from ingesting the light of so many stars. They needed a greater source of power. That's when the Luminous Beings decided to sacrifice themselves and their star, the brightest star in the cosmos, and infuse their light into the Supreme Crystal."

"And they … they're all dead now?" Oona stammered, her heart heavy.

Eterna bent her head toward her, looking at her with infinite tenderness.

"Almost all of them, *min tolthae*. They had to make sure that the crystal would not be used for the wrong ends, and decided to hide it on Earth in order to protect me. They knew they could trust me to carry on their mission. But, threatened by Astera's rapidly increasing power, they didn't have time to give me the sacred gem directly. They were worried that it might fall into the wrong hands and hurriedly hid three of their children on Earth, giving each of them a fragment of the map that would guide them to the Supreme Crystal."

Oona felt like she'd swallowed a hedgehog. She had trouble understanding Eterna's words and looked at her, dumbfounded.

"You mean that we … that I …?" Oona stammered, her cheeks growing hot.

The goddess stared at Oona, her large eyes fringed with decorative grasses, and nodded.

"It's not easy, what I'm trying to tell you. You're not human. Well, not completely. You are a Luminous Being."

"What?" Nawal jumped in, her eyes wide.

Despite the circumstances, Oona just managed to refrain from hiccupping with laughter. She had always had this nervous reflex in the middle of bizarre, sometimes tragic, situations. Eterna, meanwhile, remained impassive. Oona got a hold of herself and shuddered.

"A Luminous Being? You mean I'm … an extraterrestrial?" she asked in a tiny voice, struggling against the dizziness that was threatening to overwhelm her.

Oona couldn't feel her body, her ears were ringing, and the ground seemed to be giving way beneath her. The goddess had a serious expression. Oona had often hoped to one day find out that she'd been adopted, but to go from that to thinking of herself as an extraterrestrial …

"But I don't have blue skin …" she murmured. "Neither do Nawal or Aqiwo."

"Skin color depends only on the angle of exposure to the sun. You have white skin on Earth and blue skin in the Milky Way, but if you were to visit the next galaxy and got closer to their sun, your skin would turn violet. The closer you are to the sun, the darker your skin. Conversely, the farther away you are, the lighter your skin becomes. But your inner light never changes."

"But if I'm a Luminous Being … who are my parents??" she gasped.

"What about mine?" Nawal chimed in, dumbfounded, running her fingers over her arm as if seeing the color of her skin for the first time.

"Oona, it was your father who hid you on Earth. Your real father."

Oona could hardly breathe. Her heart stopped beating.

"As for your real mother, she sacrificed her light to give it to the Supreme Crystal. She died, but her love for you was so strong that she passed it on to a star. If you open your heart and look up at the sky, you're sure to find her. She and I are constantly keeping watch over you, *min tolthae*."

Her star! So that's why it would flicker! It was actually her real mother! Oona felt dizzy as she took in all this information, unable to fully absorb these extraordinary revelations.

Eterna turned to Nawal, who was also having trouble processing what she'd just heard.

"Your parents were infinitely good, and they also passed on their light to the Crystal. Like Oona, you are one of my children, and you'll be able to feel their love whenever you look up at the starry sky. Along with Oona's father, the three of you are all that's left of the Luminous Beings' civilization."

The reference to Aqiwo distressed Oona. Her eyes glistened with tears as she looked at his motionless body.

"And how are we going to save Aqiwo?"

"All you have to do is use your power."

Oona immediately stopped crying and bounded to her feet, as if propelled by a spring. She walked over to where Aqiwo laid under a lotus tree, covered in pink blossoms.

"Really? I can bring Aqiwo back to life?! What should I do?" she almost shouted. *Could it possibly be true!?*

Eterna handed the Supreme Crystal to Oona.

"*Ohr te ni, Ngalathaer Nilhil*" [O Sacred Source, may your power be revealed], Eterna sang deferentially. "Oona, hold the crystal in one hand and place the other on Aqiwo's chest."

She did as she was instructed. Suddenly, Aqiwo's body began to give off a bluish light. Oona gave a small cry of surprise. Faint, sapphire-colored lines appeared in the foliage of the majestic tree, like luminous veins running through its leaves. Eterna knelt and gazed with a worried expression at the boy's motionless face.

"Aqiwo needs more light to come back to us. Oona, can you try harder?"

Oona dug down deep to invoke the forces of Nature. A violet light gradually spread throughout the boy's body and the luminescent tree. Yet his body remained still. Without taking her eyes off him, Oona increased her efforts. She was holding her breath as she held her glowing hand on her friend's chest. The lack of oxygen gave her a headache. It felt like a vise was crushing her skull into a thousand pieces. She fought against the pain with all her might as beads of sweat rolled down her forehead. At last, the boy opened his eyes and blinked, looking confused.

"Aqiwo!" she exclaimed.

"Am I …?" he mumbled weakly, looking up.

Oona threw her arms around his neck and embraced him with all her might. Now, her friend's eyes were glowing with a miraculous fire.

The lotus began to sparkle with bursts of purple light.

"You gave us such a scare!" admonished Oona, weeping with joy.

A smile played on Aqiwo's lips.

"He needs to rest now," the goddess warned as she placed the Supreme Crystal back inside her flowering heart.

"Eterna … my mother … on Earth? Can I save her too? Will I see her again?" she asked excitedly.

"Yes, *min tolthae*, your earthly mother was aware of your real identity. She loved you as her own daughter, and that love will never disappear. You can see her again whenever you want."

Oona looked at Eterna and then at her star in the sky, which was blinking wildly as if it approved of the Earth spirit's words. Mystified, Oona beamed. She had always felt so alone and yet, suddenly, she had acquired three mothers, a father, two friends, and two guides. And nature would always be there for her. Oona's heart swelled with gratitude at the thought of her new family!

Oona blinked in disbelief and stretched her hands toward Eterna, as if to embrace her. The deity smiled at her, and a wave of comfort coursed through her body. Within the sphere, the Dark Cloud lifted its veil from the precious planet Earth to reveal myriads of snow-capped mountain ranges and vast oceans of pure water. Oona stifled a cry of amazement, then grabbed Aqiwo's hand. The light of a new dawn was illuminating the Earth from the farthest reaches of the cosmos. The young boy lifted his head toward Eterna, his golden eyes sparkling like two diamonds.

"The forest of my ancestors! Has it been saved?"

Buds opened in Eterna's abundant hair, which was adorned with a thousand leaves.

"Most of your family's trees were spared," the goddess declared, shaking her verdant hair.

The leaves that covered her flowering hair swirled in the air before scattering to the ground around Aqiwo.

"Can I see them?" he asked excitedly, before falling back breathlessly onto his makeshift bed.

"And my father and brother?" cried Nawal, her eyes tearful.

"They returned home safely. I will help you teleport there if you like," Eterna offered pleasantly. "As for you, Aqiwo, you are still too weak. You need to regain your strength first."

The boy frowned and, with what appeared to be a superhuman effort, obediently laid still, his jaw clenched.

"What if I go and see the forest of Aqiwo's ancestors?" Oona suggested. "And then I can also visit my mother! I mean my earthly mother," she stammered, still struggling to process all recent events.

At the thought of her earthly mother, she felt a lump of sadness in her throat.

Eterna gazed at Oona with a look that was both tender and concerned.

"Thothan can take you there. But be careful, *min tolthae*, for the threads of light are still fragile. Astera didn't succeed in killing me, but my life force has waned. Let's hope that this time she remains forever confined to the black hole that drew her in."

Oona's jaw dropped in surprise and she glanced at her companions, hanging on Eterna's every word.

"You mean the Earth is still in danger?" Aqiwo asked worriedly.

"Even though Asura has been destroyed, her Cloud has not entirely dissipated … Not all humans have been reconnected to my heart," the deity sighed, her luxuriant curls turning into bare tree branches, as if the victims of a harsh winter. "Alas, as long as the Cloud remains, the dark forces will always threaten the Earth and the stars in the cosmos."

Staring at the small blue globe revolving in an ocean of stars at the center of the sphere, Oona realized that this meant the fight wasn't over.

"And when are we going to see you again?" Oona asked, a sense of loss gnawing at her stomach.

Eterna's strength and kindness had comforted her on all the journeys and through all the trials of the past few days, her maternal presence giving the young girl a sense of security she hadn't felt in a long time. She felt deeply attached to the spirit of the Earth and she couldn't imagine no longer having her as part of her life. Oona rushed toward Eterna's hair and hugged a small tree as if clutching a treasure to her heart. Her nose was tickled by scents of moss and rosewood mixed with notes of pine. A thousand daisies suddenly bloomed in the shrub's foliage.

"Don't worry, my child. Three nights from now, I will meet you in the meadow of Aqiwo's ancestors beneath the Big Dipper. You can decide then if you wish to continue your journey with me."

Relieved, Oona loosened her grip.

"Meanwhile, I will call other children to be Guardians of the Earth in order to help me protect the filaments of light," the goddess continued. "Like you, these children, had to face extraordinary difficulties and endure great loneliness."

"Are they also Luminous Beings?" asked Nawal with a look of amazement.

"These children are humans. They are the Forgotten Ones," Eterna concluded.

CHAPTER XXI
The Grass Dance

Oona was determined to honor the promise she'd made to Aqiwo. She clung to Thothan's feathers as he dove toward the forest of Aqiwo's ancestors. As the cool air stung her cheeks, she felt as if her fingers were melting in the eagle's fluffy down. Down below, her eye was caught by a truck driver stopping his vehicle at the edge of the forest. The dull expression in his eyes brightened and the Earth was reflected in his irises. He seemed to be outraged as he gazed at the corpses of dead trees littering the ground around him. Another driver joined him and shook his head at the sight of the green cadavers. Deeper in the forest, all the harvesting machines were turning around. "Aqiwo's sacred forest is saved!" Oona rejoiced inwardly. She raised her arms as a sign of victory, narrowly escaping from falling. Thothan turned his head toward Oona and gave her a knowing glance. She stretched forward and kissed the eagle's silky neck feathers; he seemed to smile in contentment.

Three days later, Oona was looking forward to seeing Aqiwo before their meeting with Eterna. The huge white bird dropped Oona off in front of the bus stop and then flew away toward Althaleia, his wings flapping loudly. As humans had realized that they needed to protect nature, the new school bus didn't have any wheels and was flying over the road. The electric vehicle glided nimbly through the air toward Oona and then the door slid silently open, allowing her to board. There was no longer a driver behind the wheel! But where was Ms. Daniels? Oona worried that perhaps she'd been fired. She leaned inside the vehicle cautiously and quivered with joy at the sight of Aqiwo who was sitting at the back of the capsule, waiting for her. She ran toward him.

"Aqiwo! Are you feeling better?"

"Yes, I've completely recovered," he stated confidently. "And what about you? Have you been to visit your mother?"

Oona's heart swelled with joy, somewhat mitigated by guilt.

"Yes, she's doing much better!" she said, brightly. "But I can't help thinking that if I'd just discovered my powers earlier, if I'd been stronger, I might have been able to save her sooner," she added, shaking her head.

Aqiwo's golden pupils flashed out a warning.

"Oona, how can you say such a thing? You're barely eleven years old!"

Her friend's thoughtful remark eased her mind. Deep down, she also felt guilty for constantly thinking about her star in the sky, her real, her Luminous, mother. She felt like she was betraying her earthly mother, who had always encouraged her to continue looking into her celestial origins.

"And I saw your forest! The trees of your ancestors are saved!"

Aqiwo's chest rose like a tidal wave, and he let out a long sigh of relief. Emotional, he wiped away a tear that was forming at the edge of his black lashes.

"Look."

He showed her a small painting in faded colors that he'd been holding on his lap. Half a dozen Chumash people were dancing in a circle around a campfire.

Oona recognized the small rectangular object that Aqiwo had fiercely protected from the naughty monkey when they were receiving their kung fu training on Althaleia.

"What is it?" she asked.

"This is a painting of my parents. That's them here," he said, pointing to a young couple in traditional costume. "And here, you see, is my grandmother, the chief of the tribe! There's even my dog, White Hawk, when he was just a few months old, the same age I was at the time," he said, pointing to the little white ball of fur at the edge of the dancing circle. "The forest is sacred to us because we come from trees, and we become trees again when we go through the Great Passage. The trees are my family, Oona," declared the Guardian of the Forests. "Do you understand?"

"Yes, I think so," she murmured, moved.

"This is the only image I have of them and I never want to lose it."

"They're so lovely! They look like birds," she said, admiringly.

Aqiwo looked nostalgic as a smile spread across his face.

"I can teach you to dance like them if you like," he suggested, blinking shyly.

Oona felt a wave of excitement course through her.

"Oh yes, I'd love that!"

"Tonight, in the meadow, if you want?"

"Yes, we could meet up a little bit before we're supposed to meet Eterna. Oh, look!" she suddenly exclaimed.

Outside, a procession of monks draped in yellow robes was approaching the school bus on foot. Above them, a giant billboard was plastered with a picture of Ms. Daniels, now apparently the star of a glamorous Hollywood production. So, her dream had come true after all! Oona felt so happy for her. One of the monks uncovered their head. The face that was lifted up towards them was … Master Wada's. Oona and Aqiwo met the Venerable Elder's gaze. The nun bowed and smiled conspiratorially at them. What was she doing there? Would Master Wada be at the meeting that night? Oona suspected that their adventures were far from over.

At nightfall, the meadow of Aqiwo's ancestors was lit by the dancing light from a campfire that was burning a few feet away. Aqiwo, wearing a headdress with brightly colored feathers, was kneeling in the meadow, looking at his laptop. White Hawk was sitting next to him, howling and staring at the moon. Impressed by his splendid, feathered headdress, Oona felt a mixture of excitement and trepidation, along with a faint desire to laugh at the incongruity of the situation. She bit her lip, holding back a nervous hiccup. Dressed in a fringed tunic with beaded embroidery that she'd found in a Chumash store, and with her hair pulled back by a feathered headband, she smoothed her dress and approached her friend.

The sound of tribal drums rose into the air. The sacred trees of Aqiwo's ancestral forest surrounded them with their comforting presence, emitting scents of sandalwood and pine. Aqiwo's face, the color of polished amber, turned toward her and a golden light blazed in his eyes. *He's so handsome!* Oona thought, breathlessly. He stood up and reached his hand out toward her. An unknown feeling tied her stomach into knots. Gazing at his open hand, she pressed her palm against his, thrilling inwardly at his touch. The skin on her forearms prickled and her heart raced, bursting into a strange melody.

"Do you feel the music?" murmured the young boy, moving his feet to the rhythm of the drums.

Oona nodded as she raised first her right foot and then her left foot in imitation of his movements. But she knew she was just marching on the spot, stiff as a post, and she cursed her awkwardness. He must think she was ridiculous! Her cheeks flushed and she prayed he wouldn't notice her turmoil.

"Move like the grass blowing in the breeze …" he continued, pressing his warm hand against hers.

Despite herself, Oona giggled nervously. The dancing flames projected shadows onto Aqiwo's face, and his eyes enveloped her with infinite tenderness. Suddenly feeling very embarrassed, she lowered her gaze.

"This is the grass dance," he explained as Oona tried to concentrate.

The drumbeats now dissolved into a soft symphony of flutes. Aqiwo pulled her to him, encouraging her to put her hands around his neck.

"You see, the grass is swaying with us," he murmured softly.

Their faces were almost touching. The sudden proximity released a cascade of thrills inside her, making it impossible for her to pay attention to his instructions. Oona felt her cheeks burning as the warmth in the young boy's eyes set her heart ablaze. Smitten, she rested her head on his shoulder and surrendered herself to his embrace, swaying as she gazed into the starry sky.

Just then, her star started to blink in the night, disrupting her tranquility. Oona reached her hand toward the twinkling star. "Mommy?" she asked inwardly. What had her mother looked like before she'd turned into a star? And where was her father? Did he have blue skin? Was he a hero, a good guy? And what had he been doing all those years, leaving her alone in the hands of the horrible Asura? She was hurt that he hadn't tried to find her, and a wave of emotion choked her. She suddenly had the desire to shout to the stars that she needed him, that she needed a father, a guide, a protector … when Eterna's two huge, diamond-clear eyes appeared amid the stars. A majestic white eagle circled in the air and Cosmos landed on the goddess' shoulder.

"Cosmos!" Oona shouted, bursting with joy.

Above the baby bird, the glorious deity was surrounded by a dozen bubbles, each of which contained a child. *The Forgotten Ones!* Oona's mouth fell open, but not a single word came out. She gazed at the children's faces in the shimmering bubbles, wondering what their stories were. But where was Nawal? The trees quaked as the wind roared through their branches and the blades of grass caressed her bare ankles, as if to speak to her. She felt so much love for the Earth, this little blue globe, so precious and so beautiful, that floated in an ocean of stars. It had to be protected at all costs! Eterna had explained to them that her filaments of light were still fragile, that not all humans had been reconnected to her heart. Some wouldn't hesitate to harm nature, putting the planet in danger once more. What dangers were still threatening all of them?

A flood of questions raced through her mind. She tightened her arms around Aqiwo's neck as if to drive these thoughts away and enjoy this final moment with him. Cosmos nestled his head against her cheek. She smiled blissfully. As she contemplated the night sky and the shimmering bubbles, she said to herself that now, at last, she was no longer alone.

Oriane Livingston

Oriane Livingston is a critically acclaimed French American published novelist, filmmaker and environmentalist.

A graduate from UCLA School of Law and a former attorney, her love for books and movies compelled her to embrace an artistic career. Throughout her journey, she's had the privilege of collaborating on numerous films with several Academy Award winning film producers and studios in Hollywood and in Europe.

Her storytelling aims at reconnecting us to the natural world. She draws her inspiration from wild animals, trees and stars.

A nature lover, Oriane can often be found on the hiking trails of the Santa Monica Mountains in Los Angeles with Cosmos, her beloved husky. Like Oona, she is a vegan and a meditator.

The Guardians of Earth is her second novel. Visit www.orianelivingston.com for more.